DIALOGUES WITH THE MASTERS

by

Lori M. Poe

A Hearthstone Book

Carlton Press, Inc. New York, N.Y.

Other books by Lori M. Poe

Dynamic Keys to Self Discovery

Wake Up and Walk with God

Manufactured in the United States of America
ISBN 0-8062-2351-0

To Every Soul
That Would Listen
To The Voice Of
The Inner Master

Introduction

This poetic, God-inspired book of soul talks between Master and pupil is a compilation of spiritual teachings received over thirty years. Long ago, when I accepted Heaven's Shining Invitation, my weightless spirit tapped into a Great Network of Sound, Color and Light, that scooped me up and brought me straightaway to the Foot of the Master where the pen of my heart recorded the text.

This book holds no promise for quick success, for you shall be the Promise fulfilled as you yield to the precepts of regeneration that translate into spiritual freedom and longevity under the Guiding Spirit of God. Truth, Comfort and Love all-abiding shall linger on in an unbroken, personal way long after you have layed this light-filled book aside.

Hierarchical Masters resound a powerful Message to earth, whether to servant, seeker, teacher, or to the restless wanderer who roams from life to life, age to age, in the Holy Quest of God-Realization, their messages are vital to every step of spiritual unfoldment and wholesome living. Positive instructions from Master to pupil link the soul to spiritual progress, Sound and Light, provide the stabilizing equations that re-establish inner and outer balance to the seeker. The Ascended Master imbues the heart with inspiration, innovation, creativity, and new incentives that call for regeneration and soul-building in view of the bright, new destiny that beckons from far off sky-blue horizons.

Cosmic road-signs point to sunlit Worlds of God, where cities lay in the golden-white glow of Spiritual Worlds, where cosmic foothills, mountain valleys, seas, and vast continents bathe in the glories of a sparkling New Morning and mountains wrapped in Eternal Light shoulder high into the blue-white brilliance of Cosmic Altitudes. Benevolent as the illuminated way shines forth to the soul, stern admonishments in the precepts of regeneration may not be too palatable to the sensitive being, but the results are utter peace, release from anxieties, poverty and dis-ease. Then you shall truly be rich and all you do bear a blessing. Perhaps the noble scholar may find directive dialogues too elementary, but the Emissaries of God speak in simplicity and in Power.

They speak softly, distinctly, without flattery, their dispensations are given gradually, by degree, according to what each soul can absorb and utilize. With consent, the Master-Light blots out old concepts that are replaced with the shining newness of a cleansed heart. Wayshowers of Perfection that speak to you through the spirit of my book, bring you into the natural alignment to the Law, the Lord, and into the Light of illumination and self-discipline; that the Oil of Love may erase the moanings of human distress and filter in a courage and strength that sustains daily, hourly and momentarily. The audible Sound of the Word enables you to feel the all-abiding God Presence of the Master that lifts you into God-Reality of which you are a part.

The rugged, simple way to God is paved with self-discipline, steadfast application of Divine Order to every facet of life and living in balanced detachment that reveals the Vision of God more clearly. After set forth conditions have been met, the mind becomes as a crystal clear mirror that reflects Divine Intent in every way. Then you shall no longer fear the wooden path of sorrow, for the Light illumines your footpath, the Invisible becomes visible and perpetual protection prevails.

The heart of every man is a shrine, the purified soul a magnetic attraction to which Divine Love is drawn. Many souls upon earth feel a sense of isolation during their temporary exile in human form, but the Living Spirit that permeates every page of this book shall break and shatter every chained feeling of loneliness and separatedness, for you no longer walk alone. Teachings of the Spheres flow down into lower worlds on electronic bands of Light through the audible Lifestream that is Life to all creation, universes and worlds without end. Ascended Masters and Angelic Beings carry their Flaming Torch of Wisdom into the earth world to illumine the soul of humanity. The audible Melody trails like a thousand strings through inner chambers of the sacred soul, thus it finds the crowning glory of a brand New Dawn. Communication is of the Spirit, it is Love Ethereal and Forever.

Soft Sounds of Cosmic Marimbas shall lift you into the Reality of your True Self and the symphony of your being shall compose a new song, born of inner content in a life that is free, noble and God-directed; as you follow the precepts in regeneration under the Guardianship of the Overshadowing Master.

Come, Blessed Friend, draw your cloak of Light closer around your shoulder and journey with me into Cosmic Dimensions to hear the Dialogues with the Masters as you turn to Chapter One.

I wish you God-speed and *LOVE*!

"Having many things to say unto you, I would not write with paper and ink; but I trust to come unto you and speak face to face that your joy may be full." (Second Epistle of John, vs. 12)

Contents

DIALOGUES WITH THE MASTERS

Chapter One

Angels, Guardians, and Masters, the Instructors of Man

All sacred scriptures give evidences and attestments to the valid Reality of Invisible Helpers, the Guardians that care for every incarnate individuality upon earth, on other planets, universes in Higher World Reality and for all existing lifewaves that slowly move through evolutionary cycles toward God-Realization.

Our immediate guardian is the Light within the soul, beyond this inborn Light-Force are hosts of Angels and celestial Beings that guard, protect, instruct and counsel us until we are ready to set foot upon the shining way of God-Realization through soul travel. The slow upward climb demands adherence to the Precepts of Regeneration that lay the foundation to further unfoldment.

Holy succor is available at all times whether or not we can reconcile to this fact. Since time immemorial individual man has called upon Divine aid and intercession, especially when life seemed on the rocks and the weary wanderer felt the strain of being stranded upon the shifting sands of human existence. There he began to trust in a celestial Helper that he instinctively believed would be more qualified than himself to keep him out of harm's way and upon whom he could more confidently depend, whereas before he endured constant letdowns of misplaced trust in his brother man, he could now look to brighter horizons.

Even though Angels and Invisible Helpers may lighten the weight of a burden and certainly lift the veil obscuring man's clearer perception to see the cause of his problems, at times the Holy Being blocks pathways when the unwilling one refuses to mend its way, in order to bring body, soul and spirit into more harmonious rapport through change. This means we are left to our own undoing, to prove the way out of misery is from within, requiring inner fortitude to work out our own problems. Becoming self-emptied and God-contained changes conditions around us for great betterment. When life seems at its lowest point and obstacles insurmountable, the Guiding Force walks ever so near. It takes but a moment to enter the silence where no storm can touch or anything harm, to realize the Radiant Being of the Inner Master, the Holy Spirit and unfailing Helper. Its rays shine into the soul and flood the whole being with new vitality, renewed enthusiasm and wonderfully uplifting ideas. This change of vibrations issues forth a new attitude concerning all things, inner and outer conditions come into balance and life again takes on a rosy glow.

Touched by Angelic Virtue, everything becomes astoundingly clear. Often the meeting lasts but a second but in that moment soul is satisfied and can accept the Will and Love of the Governing Power, no matter what pain or hindrances may have tried it to the last. Such holy encounters bring forth our best qualities, excellence and the impulse to simply do what is right.

No man can defer us from doing what we choose. No one is ever left to fate, for soul is the very part of God, a part of the Great Plan to which a portion and responsibility is assigned. Concerning this, Epictetus explained to his doubting friend: "Thou art the sun! in thine orbit thou hast power to make the year and the season; to bid the fruits of earth increase, the winds arise and fall....go, make the cicuit, and thus minister unto all from the greatest to the least." Herewith we also see that every human task, no matter how small, menial or insignificant it may seem, plays a most vital role in the Workings of God when it is rendered ungrudgingly and in love. It is the spirit in which we perform our duties that makes them wonderful or accursed.

Invisible helpers and angels are never a crutch since it is most important to them that we learn self-reliance and exercise our will and energy constructively. If we are too troubled to still the mind to perceive the sound and light of their force, then the Angel works through another soul attuned to Him to bring us into His aid or directly releases our need to the Inner Master, the Holy Spirit and speedy enlightment is given. At times a friend or a stranger becomes a vehicle of Spirit, brings to you the archetype of Angelic thought that points into better directions.

Angels, Masters and Beings of Light are our brothers and

sisters. They are not to be worshipped but revered. The God-Country where they reside is within you. You recognize it through inner experience only, where you see all realms and Heaven-Worlds interblending and overlapping with inner and outer reality. How? Through out-of-body consciousness and soul travel, that is the way. Once the soul has entered this state of God-Consciousness while still in physical embodiment, it may live in a continued state of Grace while on earth and feel the blessing, by its own good choice to live the spiritual life. When you feel that inner nudging of stern thought, of correcting, warning, even foretelling in a vision or dream, these are not human imagination but Divine Guidances to redirect your life.

Even though you see Divine Beings seemingly on the outer, it is experienced positively on the Inner through your spiritual unfoldment, all vision, every experience, every baptism and intitiation take place *WITHIN*.

Of this, Stopford A. Brook said: "No angels come to us! No celestial voices speak to us! Oh, believe it not. Every deep impression of rightness of an action, every keen conviction of a truth, every inward cry for light and impulse onward, are messengers, voices of God."

My experiences proved angelic radiances to be of various effulgence, different colors and energy empowerments. Once an Angel veiled in a wonderful light blue mist appeared to my inner sight. At the time I didn't think of angels but prayed for a neighbor. All the more my surprise to behold His large, soulful eyes shining into my devotions. Shortly thereafter a very trying, painful condition was removed from the one prayed for. After this happening when an insoluble circumstance came before me, I would contemplate on the Angel of the Blue Mist and usually someone's burden became lighter.

An Angel of apricot Radiance appears to us when we are ready to begin a certain mission or one draws to a close as it was in my experience. The First was the appearance of an Angel in shining armor and unmentionable beauty. My body was so supercharged with His pale orange rays and bathed in electromagnetic warmth, that when I turned off the light, the bulb blew out of the socket and pulverized before I touched the lamp. The second Appearance of the Divine One was just as beautiful, but saddened me, for as He revealed Himself to Me, I suddenly instinctively knew a work was coming to a close. It was so, but replaced by a much better way of service.

Angels of Love and Healing can be seen in your place of worship or healing room. You can perceive their enormous outlines against the wall even running into the footage of the ceiling. The radiance of cherubs are sometimes seen as a circular brightness of rainbow colored lights, their lovely features are clearly discernible, though they as all the other Beings are veiled as not to insure the human eye with their brilliance. Even the Glorious Light that appears in the midst of your mental screen or meeting a Lord of another Dimension can be so bright it hurts the Inner Eye. Yet protection prevails. Think of the Light that came to St. Paul on the road to Damascus. It is one and the same Light, would God give it to one and not to another?

By your own efforts to regenerate on every level, you grow accustomed to the pristine brightness of Heavenly Spheres.

At times visitors tell me of feeling penetrating heat as they step into the healing room. I call it the 'Spirit of the Place.' I've noticed this Presence does not permit undesirables to enter. In one instance a person's car would not turn the corner to enter the street. On second attempt the car would not stop and the party passed up the building. On third, the individual felt profound vibrations and gave up. I was totally unaware of this happening until I was told about it. The accounts of spiritual protection would make for a large book. Angels overshadow every prayerful activity. The scripture refers to the Angel saying: "Behold, I send an Angel before thee, to keep you in the way and to bring thee into the place which I have prepared." (Exodus 23:20)

Divine Counsel is never withheld, we should open our hearts to receive deeper insights of the Realities of God's Shining Host.

The Visitation

Angelic Messages of Sound and Light drop into the listening soul like pebbles into a quiet pond. It happened long ago in the deep silent hour of a Christmas Night. A gentle Voice aroused me from sleep in penetrating sound: "Awake, and WRITE!" The soft echo of the Voice lingered in my head, first I thought it to be part of a dream, especially since writing was the worst chore I could think of, so I asked: "Write what?" but an inner urgency persisted. I grumbled and reluctantly struggled to arise. I squinted at the clock, it was three a.m. I dropped into the chair by my desk and yawned in displeasure, asking: "Lord, what would Thou have me do?" Pondering the unreality of the Voice I fumbled for pad and pen, just in case! I felt an enveloping soft melody round about, perceived a presence standing to my left, my skin crawled in fright. Oh yes, it snapped me promptly into wakefulness! I beheld a softly shimmering Light to my left. Undecided whether to jump up, run or stay, a sudden slight pressure of that unknown Presence engulfed me in tranquility, my fingers drew like magnets to pencil and pad and the pen of my heart began to record in rapid dictation that formed into the text.

A strange Power drew me into the weightlessness of Spirit, where my thinking became clear and sharp and I understood more than words could ever express. My pen continued to record many dictations of the Inner Master. All sound around me ceased, even the old clock on the wall had stopped ticking away. And then, the sounding voice faded, I had come back from a journey into Light, the Master had gone as quickly as He came. And wherever He might have gone I wanted to be there also. He couldn't be too far off, I thought, for I still felt His all-abiding Presence as my tears dripped over the paper, for: "I was in the spirit on the Lord's Day and heard behind me a great voice, saying: what thou seest, write in a book, write the things which thou hast seen, and the things which are, and things which shall be thereafter." (Rev. 1:10-11-19)

A feeling of longing, almost like homesickness befell me. Often I burned the midnight oil until early dawn, contemplating the Master's Presence, waiting for Him to come to teach me. Sometimes He did, other times I sat waiting into the hush of night, felt the brush of Angel Wings draw near, Masters, Initiators, Holy Guardians too, who taught me the Ways of God. At times I was lifted to sunlit lands, to worlds beautiful beyond description, words fail me. Over the years many dictations came forth, at other times I sat at the Master's Feet in the Realities of God and jotted down as I remembered, seldom losing even a single word. Some of these pearls are shared with you in this book. Should the Voice of the Inner Council seem too harsh or stern to my discerning Reader, it is only because my life called for much discipline and even more needed to come into submission in the face of the work Spirit layed out for me. Truth is seldom kind but in the end it shall be to us the Rose of Attainment. It was a lifelong quest this search of God, may it be profitable and uplifting to everyone sharing in His teachings through the Dialogues with the Masters.

Masterly Directions

So I gathered up the Words of the Master in White, Who dropped them into the cradle of my heart and tried to reassemble them in the simplicity they were received. Truly, as flowers gathered up on a winding mountain trail, I put them into a bouquet as best I could. Often He came to take me on journeys to Inner Lands, even though my hand kept recording, the soul went into Cosmic Dimensions. I lived in both worlds if not in all. It was a magic moment when I stood at the kitchen sink wahing dishes, when the Voice came into being and Sounds of Love that felt as a cool rushing wind from Inner Worlds, gave me a new name, and called me thus from then on.

"Rose-Hanna," spoke He to me: "Consider many things, foremost the Realities of the Kingdom of God! Consider the narrow, liberating path leading each soul into its own awareness to the heights of God-Realization. We show the way to God's Holy Mountain of Light, walk in it! Let thy testimony be perfect and moral that mortal strength be reborn through spiritual living, then the Redeemer shall quicken the light and blot out the shadow of thy being. Allow not the tempter who cometh in human flesh to deter thee from thy destined goal, for verily he shall come in many guises. Let thy speech reflect a spirit of charity, truth, hope, and lovingkindness, even when hardship lies across the way. I say, behold *LOVE* in the small and mighty, speaking rightly to all that would hear. Keep thyself in Sound and Light it is thy Inner Being that balance would remain in the golden triad and conform not ungodliness when want and lack test to the last; for all who serve shall learn thankfulness in what is being provided for the moment, that true riches may be realized. Soon the Living Christ shall be reborn in every heart and He shall enter into thy holy tabernacle and not forsake thee that thy joy may be full.

"Beloved Heart, fall not into they former estate of superficial thinking lest ye lose what was garnered. The time has come to thee to serve a greater cause and when sharp, winding curves of the long God-Trail take thy breath, deviate not from the narrow, for when the gaze is fixed upon the smaller self in pity, it distorts the vision of a destiny that must be fulfilled; the veil of Maya must be shattered before ye can see the road map clear!

"My Scribe, rewards are given when thy works are rendered in the Name of God, small efforts beget great compensation time after time when ye persist in steadfastness, doing good. Tasks must be worked out to optimum perfection if ye would benefit the World-Soul and the whole. Say not: 'The Lord hast forsaken me,' when dark hours of test and trial assail thee, for I AM with thee in the Christ of God. Only in thy steadfast belief are thine enemies brought to naught, they become friends when ye hold the tongue, guard thy thoughts and ever look to Him, Whose cross was yet more painful." Again the Voice fell silent.

The Mountain of Light

I pondered the Master's Words, this first, short heart-to-heart talk, and avowed to do my best. Since I withdrew into periodic solitude of quiet living in search of Truth that seemed veiled from many, my hours were filled with meditations, supplications and active contemplation to prepare myself for further dictations from the Master. Some of my acquaintances whose emptiness seemed large at times and who knew more about preparation than silence of Spirit, found me 'sick' and very strange for I respectfully declined their invitations and no longer desired carousing around. I was gone on my silent treasure hunts and glad nobody cared. New friends understood and once in a while I would sigh; "What price, Emancipation?" At the same time I couldn't explain my inner happiness, it was bigger than anything I knew; because I had stumbled unto something so magnificent, in fact overwhelming! One moment my feet were on earth while in the next my footless spirit would go on journeys of discovery where I found cosmic settings of breathtaking, wondrous country sites, where mountain valleys and Cosmic foothills were undefiled and pure. I entered cities bathed in spiritual Light, teeming with activities, where hamlets shone in heavenly effulgence, bird songs diffused the air and meadows lay studded with riots of exotic blooms, what glorious Lands above the stars! Children played, sang and danced, people in love walked hand in hand along green promenades and sparkling waterfalls proved to me that Heaven was a Land of Life and action, at least in Heaven's lower spheres and fourth-dimensional altitude.

It was as though a flame of holy passion was kindled in me by an Unseen Hand; I realized a Love that cannot be found except in Him, and for that Love I could do anything, or try. When the magnetic pull of a loving force moved the soul into action to experience the Great Beyond, I received the jewel by which I could break through Inner Gates to go where souls learn to love better and I entered Temples of Instruction to study the hallowedness of life and proper application of spiritual energies entrusted to me. My fruitless idleness came to a certain end and the new path dawning before me brought me to regret the hours I had spent in self-warming love.

By a sensation of weightlessness, warm Cosmic Sunrays found me at the foot of God's Holy Mountain, waiting for my Noble Instructor. Heavenly fragrances of ethereal blooms, ardor of rose and lilac swished around my head, fanned the golden flame of my heart into gleaming brightness. Oh, I wished I could stay here forever! Now stood my First Initiator upon soft meadowed ground in radiant Light, His Face bore the smile of the Gods. A vibrating brightness of His majestic Aura pulled my thoughts upward as He commandingly raised His gnarled staff:

"Rose-Hanna, My Scribe, record well! From etheric Gardens we behold man upon earth in search of a Great Truth. I say, the spiritual life is not acquired in subtle manner, but in fearlessness, patience, obedience, spiritual allegiance and well-balanced seeking, soul shall reach the pristine landscapes of its noble estate. Soul's Holy Mountain is the mountain of self-discipline, overcoming, not by force but by detachment from vice, vengeance and self-hate. This regeneration brings the Arhat nearer the Zenith of perfection, albeit he would release his being to Holy Powers, his attitudes and self-will. Each must scale the towering heights by himself, none may borrow, none may lend that the Law of Love be fulfilled to the letter and soul may see the Mountain of Light in all Reality that stands as a crystal palace in the shining Voltage of Spirit.

"I say, Super-Consciousness gives admittance to the pilgrim who enters through the open door in orderly fashion, else he must retrace his steps until the right is again earned, the next step may again be taken. How deeply man is capable of impersonal loving, how well he knows to separate the self from physical and material bondage determines how well he shall climb. Yet he is not alone though the road is hard and lonely; for the Star of Hope is his Wayshower on his ascent into the light of final liberation.

Contemplation leads him into the God-Way where the Star's magnetic qualities draw to the purity of the traveler's cloak, giving to each its own reflection. The climber is witness to a great pilgrimage, beholds others ascending through the Mists, yet each climbs alone. He who responds to the Melodies of soul carries into the God-Worlds, he clearly beholds the Light that shineth amidst the throng. Some labor for lifetimes to regain their noble estate, only the keeper of secrets shall enter the Temples of Truth. Through the Mists their pillared whiteness becomes visible to him who nears the top of God's Holy Mountain. To some the Temple of Truth is far, to others it is near. From the Ocean of Love and Mercy the melodic Sound and liberating Light echo in oneness the Call to worlds below: 'Come ye apart, come hither, I shall receive you unto Myself!' He calleth once, yea, twice, a hundredfold, but man perceiveth Him not.

"When the Christed Jewel glistens to the pilgrim's embrace, he may soar as an eagle to live in Eternity NOW, for the soul has become a Brother of the Leaf and the Force that IS aids its highest aspirations to guide others unto the path of spiritual freedom.

"Record well, My Scribe; One who ascends the spiraling dimensions unlawfully is ignorant of the fact that the Way to the Eternal is easy and swift without curves! He who willingly submits to the tutelage of a black master and adulterates his glory in black craft, dark night shall befall his passing. His grueling actions of yore and pitiless magic shall be meted unto him again, aye, I say, by the fangs of his own black master! He faces a hard redemption if allowed to reenter another life upon earth where only a dedicated life of humble service and the Inner Master can redeem him. Though his cries are heard they remain unanswered until a later date. And though he serves and suffers in his own undoing, he must keep faith. The afflictions, curses, despair, and dispassionate pain he once inflicted upon others will be meted unto him by the hands of his own victims, though circumstances and surroundings differ, the stage is set with the self-same actors! Do not scoff or belittle such a one, woe unto him who fans the fires of another purification!

"Man upon earth fears death, yea, his own shadow, he has not learned to die in order to live! He turns from the Voice that guideth him, follows the chatter of pranksters, psuedo-teachers that soothsay him into the remnants of oblivion. If in seeking Truth ye gain by what ye lose, why doest thou weep and fear? Why doest thou fear at all? And in thy life of strife and gold-grubbing why doest thou bemoan how well another does, rather than doing better thyself? Truth shall not harm thee! Each lesson ye learn here and now builds a block to a new foundation for thy next existence.

"*I AM* come to instruct thee in Truth, inspiring, infiring thee in the Precepts of Cosmic Law that ye may clothe thyself in the Light of discipline and purity and forsaking all ugliness of deception that warp thy progress. Be ye faithful and pure. Walk in spiritual soundness and soundness of mind. Let warmongers that stick their noses long as broomsticks into thy business not affect thy balance with pleasure nor pain, be not favor seeking but self-contained and detached.

"Many of you feel thwarted by outward hindrances, vanity, delusion, greed and pride, thus they feel nameless dread dogging their footsteps that keeps them in uneasy suspension. Others follow false precepts that seduce them from from their noble purpose. They sit where ego wielders hold fanatical crusades against sin. I say, nothing burneth in the hells of self but pride and ego! What good is a teaching if it benefits no one and ye fall back into enchantments of darkness? Look to the Law of thy being, the Inner Self that is spun of His own Light, it is imperishable! Refrain from the weeping nostalgia of erring indoctrinations that belittle what they themselves cannot deliver, thievery and untruth percolate in their minds. Their gloomy presence drains away thy creativity! Spiritual living requires impeccable restraint from all of these. In adherence to God's Law, ye would learn practical, workable teachings by which ye may garner a glowing spiritual record and become free. Thus, ye subdue every destructive element of the lesser being and blot out every devastation of the Shadow. It is well to believe but better to experience, if what ye believe in would become a known truth!

"We, the Emissaries of the Word teach man of Love. Man

declareth his superficial love to another, uses it for a tool to dominate and infringe upon his right. Lack of Love is his lot in turn until he forsakes acrimony and deceit. Love in its Mercy feels the silent grieving of another. Love is not sanctified lest the heart can embrace it in every creature, in tender releasement dropping all pain into the Stream of Light. Until ye care for the least of these in lower worlds ye do not know Love nor charity and thy soundings are as that of a tin cup and not of the Golden Clarion. Man knows not to love, he judges, yea, belittles his brother and torments the creatures of the earth. Love feels in Mercy, blessed is he who serves without coin and whose humble estate yields to the Will of God. The time of freedom is NOW while ye are still in the flesh, not after the rest looks up to the daffodils!

"One who beholds an individual in shabby cloak, judges him derelict and strange because he liveth outside the pale of flourishing society and accepts the crumbs and drippings that fall from the tables of the rich. Aye, I say, hear ye! Such a one deprived of comforts is a pilgrim of the White Path and closer to His heart than his beholder. Man looks upon his poor brother as an outcast because his pockets are empty, washes his fingers after he dropped the alm into the poor one's hat; thus he is ignorant of the Truth, for judging the other he judges himself. The haughty know not that the poverty stricken choose his meager lot to finalize his climb upon the Mountain of Light and is closer to God than his beholder. In his plight the deprived pilgrim looks to the Ocean of Love in depth of contemplation, he is richer by far for his light-form ascends to sit at the Feast of the Gods to eat Eternal Fruit.

"Keep My Word and precepts, oh Scribe, write it into a book, so let it be! Eyes shall mist by the Touch of My Spirit, souls shall feel the Holy Succor of My Presence.

"Rest now, Rose-Hanna, this is all for this day, I shall come again. Blessings, Grace, rest upon one and all."

I AM in *CHRIST LOVE*
—Master—Y.—

My beloved Instructor had gone, rare Love trailed around me as I sat long, pondering the Words His Wisdom imparted. My heart poured out Light to the poor of the world and to the oppressor who dampens their spirit; and to those who grope hard to stomp out the Flame of Freedom, knowing deep inside that the Judge of all judges shall reduce the cornucopia of their allowance by their own measuring stick.

And I gathered up pen and pad to file this recording with all the rest, hoping the Master would soon come again.

Chapter Two

Words of the Wise and Strong

Blossoms of Encouragement

Disheartened I sat under the umbrella of shining soul-light, bewildered in the face of the strange path dawning before me. Really, what good could my little handful of service do for all the world? Was it worth it? Too hard, thought I, too much self-denial. So I penned my resignation, layed it on my desk, knowing the Noble Master would find it there. The signature of my first dictation lay irritating, burdensome on my heart and how could I compile a text when even a simple letter seemed a chore? All these and half a dozen more excuses affirmed my decision, besides, who would believe I talked to the Unseen Teacher, especially since I didn't belong to church, organization nor creed who believed only prophets could talk to God? Yet a strange urgency to do and dare prevailed.

Instead of accepting my rejection came the shining Presence of Master—Y.—. His voice trailed through the upper chambers of the soul. His stern, soulful eyes poured inspiration, consolement and encouragement through the cove of my heart.

"Child of earth," spoke the Venerable Teacher, "I am with you always! Consider the Words of Wisdom given, they do not emerge from thy mind, they are given from inner world realities. I ask but a small matter of thee, to gather up what is given and I shall direct these into channels of publication. Know then, ye are but the vessel that passes My Sayings on to be utilized by other hands, to be presented to the heart of the seeker."

For a moment I hung my head, acknowledging my vanity and selfishness, and the Master continued:

"Nay, I would not have thee walk alone in the hour of testing, nor forsake thee when tasks and probings are given. In thy heart's weariness, yea, I abide. Fear not, come to Me in silence, I walk near to all who seek Me. Be not deceived, nothing is given without price, yea, the privilege to serve must be earned. Painful learning is permitted, rewards follow and fear, doubt and inconsistency are rooted out. Mind is the gamekeeper of animalistic behavior, vice, ruthless emotions, and revenge that keep the personality on the run from itself and from the authoritive, corrective Spirit. By regenerative means of pain and desolation the heart turns inward, goes in search of the peace-giving elixir of Divine Life that every talent is used in pursuit of happiness; but when the ingenious enemy confronts, the domestic atmosphere crumbles and material difficulties arise, the wavering individual gives up the path, if not God. The archvillain never rests!

"When the sting and effect to the cause of self-imposed negation is felt, soul must free itself, regeneration must be. When the soul is unwilling to progress, the flame of Light begins purifying action that the Glory of God may again shine through. It is not that any soul should suffer but that it shall find the Hidden One expressing as its own Self. In thy works be not as those who seek to make their name illustrious by the light of another nor waste time by reading of too many books, but behold My Sayings that shall teach thee in the Way. Pridefulness, rude aggressions and to wield influence over another are the downfall of many. Honesty, humbleness, balance, and clear thinking are attributes of Spirit. Ye must become the pure vessel that brings forth Truth as ye tap the Wells of Wisdom in thy naked spirit; that He may find thee well-approved and say: 'Well done, my good and worthy servant.'

"In thine uncertainties if ye would lift thine gaze to Him, ye shall be lifted up, stand tall, strong and well rooted in Cosmos and ye shall need none other. Stronghold is found in the blossoms of prayer, contemplation, in transcending of consciousness to what IS and not to what appears to be. What ye ponder as truth is illusion and fact but not Truth! Submit thyself to the whiteness of consecration and ye shall know the happiness in life and a constant joy that shall not pale lest ye permit it. No pleasures are found in thy world of hedonistic enterprise that leads into the mire of carnality. Spirit-legging, bootlegging syndications confuse the bumbling individual, in the end he shall look down on his small world and run for sanctuary in the Promised Life of

Spirit that shall be his Fortress. Ye are never a victim of troublesome conditions, no matter how bad these appear, for ye are not the trouble, the emotion, nor the pain, but the Soul, albeit victim of thine own thoughts and actions. Soul is blameless, without beginning or end to which personality must submit its ways to become free. Listen to My Words, O Scribe, that ye may come to know the God of thy being the Formless One, that protects the soul from every peril, perilous as the journey may appear to the flesh, for as Love giveth so it taketh away and often more than ye are willing to give. But until ye let go of whimsical ideas, ideals and things, ye are in no wise ready to set foot unto the luminous Way.

"When incarnate personality denounces the darkness of Asure that coddles desire, lust, laziness, greed, and the power of materialism then the Light shall manifest, lift the shadow body and grace every pathway of soul, restore the whole being to new vitality! Ye must become master in every aspect of being if ye would vacate the wheel of repeated incarnations. My Scribe, be thanking rather than seeking favor, let thy light run out into pure dimensions and ye shall not fear fading daylight nor the shadow of the night of soul and then He shall vibrate peace and harmony through thee into all the world. Do not reason anything too greatly that appears to hamper progress, rather seek to rediscover divinity that is and the innate strength ye squandered of yore.

"Be at peace, Beloved, I abide!

"Blessings and Grace be upon one and all."

Master—Y.—

A thrill of victory filled the room as the Master's Voice fell silent. I knew He won this round and I would wait for Him again, in anticipation to pen His Teachings. Often the Noble Teacher came unannounced. Clouds of a misty, wondrous Light would come down like snowcaps on my head that infilled me with courage and the song of inspiration. Perhaps I could carry my small lantern of faith into the world of mechanical magic, for I felt the Magic of Mystical life that was better to me than what the world could give. And often I sat very still and listened to the melodic Sound of Creation in hope that the Master would again call my name and envelope me in the warmth of Cosmic Light.

Sunrays pierced the lengthening shadows of a late autumn afternoon. Kissed by the sun, treetops cast soft shadows across the lawn, swayed in the golden autumn air. A prayer of faith welled up from deep within, that Cosmic Blessedness might bring its dispensations. I sat prepared with pen and pad, my thoughts turned high to Inner Dimensions. Soon I felt a penetrating heat, my earthy pen began to record. Quiet peace infilled the soul and straightaway the outpouring brightness of the Master's Aura lifted me beyond the veils of earth upon Wisdom's Path.

"Rose-Hanna," called He to me, His penetrating clear Voice surged through my veins. "Record My Dictation, do not omit what you do not understand!

"Man must leave the door of the heart ajar to receive the living elixir of Light and Sound that feeds his understanding. Emotions must come under control! In the presence of Light earthy issues lose importance as soul begins contemplation and taps the urns of Wisdom at Inner Altars. Free from the flesh encasement soul receives the disciplines whereby enfeebling anxieties and mortal frustrations are layed to rest. Man is a spiritual being, a God becoming. Humility, balanced sacrifice and regeneration must be. Earth teachings have limited sight, the pupil becomes unwittingly involved as the lampooner leads him along the garden path that dead ends at the Gates of Shole and none dares to speak out! Sound and Light are the food of the soul, soul must break forth through the gates of consciousness to become free, to cut asunder all external idols and the teachings of demogogue. I say, be ye transformed and transmuted in the alchemy that transfigures self-willed agony, physical pain and spiritual ignorance into a life of celestial delight, that liberates from every binding shackle and mortal estate. Fear not the tempest, it cannot harm thee but only block thine pathways through thine own negations of stagnations. Albeit *I AM* with thee and *I AM* with thee beyond world's end, I cannot alter nor take away what of thine own self must be redeemed, thus reads the Law, but I trust ye would be strong. Ye must grasp the greater Vision of Infinity. Look beyond the cryptic smiles of men where the bleeding heart is seen and by the measure of progress in one and all, the Spirit of Grace shall fortify the barren field of soul and its joy shall be full.

"Ye, My Beloved, must radiate gladness amidst the birth pangs of regeneration, for sweet gladness dissolves the shadow of Asure, regeneration must be that resurrection may come! I entreat thee to enter His Silence and to move into the lighted Way of soul the grants the rose of attainment, perfection and total liberation. Accept thy duties without complaint, manual or celestial, for within thee resideth a spirit strong and wise that remains untouched by all negation, yet when ye suffer it suffers, for It is in thee and thyself in It. My Sayings are parables to some, to another they are consolation. Teachings are preceived in measure of soul's understanding. Ye find these too elementary? But I speak to all, a Teacher of many children. God is energy, soul is energy born of It, energy is never lost, how can a Soul be lost? Ye who think thyself superior to My Word, label thyself superior scribes; I shall fill thy pads with Wisdom and prove thy knowingness to naught!

"Ye who seek making commitment to the Great Cause, be prepared to labor well and to drink the bitter cup of Love to the bottom. Come ye apart, unafraid to enter the Halls of Cosmos to read the Scrolls of unwritten Mandates that ye may grow wise."

Beloved Master—Y.— stood stern, His radiant garment of White poured its brightness over Cosmic Greens, His dark eyes pentrated the soul to its core. An oscillating brilliance shone from His Noble Forehead, so bright it hurt the spiritual eyes and for a moment I had to turn away from His Glory. From deep-tanned skin shone a radiance beyond measure and the Light above His strong brows beamed in scintillating power. I sat silently waiting for further instructions. Sweet attar of Jasmin filled the air as our spirits bathed in warm Cosmic Sun. Now the Guardian of many journeys continued:

"Rose-Hanna, Blessed One, when the long journey of earth comes to finis, I abide! Long and steep is the road ahead, matters of cause and effect to be concluded. Each rung upon the Lift of Light is well merited and each pilgrim must find the Way to the Eternal alone. The help of magnetic forces and the Light of progress shine into each cause. The Sound lifts the ebony darkness that resides within all. Albeit the foot slips or whether it be a slip of the tongue, thought or action, the Golden Eye watches from the Citadel of Soul that the foggy mist obscuring Its view shall be rend' and ye shall find a new strong hold in faith.

"Ye who ascend to perfection must use good equipment and deviate not from the Shining Way of Soul, it is thine only liberation. As ye walk in the Way daily, ye shall uplift the whole for all are of one Creator, though most are unequal in divine esteem. Look to life upon earth as opportunity, a place to unburden karmic causes by which the proverb of a cross is layed down. Ye are blessed in that ye live in earth dimensions for many are waiting to enter this land of Armageddon to attain perfection.

"In thine endearing ways of commitment and troth to Him only, forsake not thy promise, for ye would feel the coarser life more than most and more painful than he who steadfastly ploughs the furrow to Spirit. We, the Teachers of Inner Courts, stand in readiness to aid and protect the seeker. Ye, who hear My Word know *I AM* with thee in this moment, so let it be! Adhere unto the Radiant Light and it shall blaze a new trail and open a Superior Way and the Floodgates of Spirit to all. And when in thy loving, giving and serving acts the Light illumines thee wholly, then ye shall also teach and guide His fold into the Life of Spiritual freedom. I say unto thee, ye are not held responsible for what ye do not know, but for what ye refused to learn and soul shall judge itself in the end in the Justice of Love. Many seek a quiet life-style, retreat into some wilderness to escape, avoid and confront the challenge of living, all else is to naught. Ye cannot run against time, and must shift back, slow and sure divinity is won, rung by rung! Ye cannot take a lazy road and win! Ye are tried in the fires of life that make perfect!

"Rose-Hanna, My Charge, behold the crystal chalice of rosy light, take and drink and be strengthened. Finis is a lesson in learning, My Grace I give unto one and all! I shall come again."

Master—Y.—

The Master had gone as quickly as He came. The exalted moments in His Presence left the soul vibrating with enlivening energies. The softly trailing Sound of His Words lingered in the cove of my heart. It felt longing sadness, but He promised to come again and I kept faith.

Unfoldment of Consciousness

Heavenly inspiration flowed into the vestibules of my being. Thoughts beamed inward, homeward into Fourth and Fifth

Dimensions. Currents of Love rippled through me in melodic waves and blazed through the realm of consciousness, where blessed Master—Y.— stood in radiant Light. By His masterly Voice turned the pages of a great book. Now spoke He to me:

"Read, Rose-Hanna, record well, My Scribe, not so many errors please! When man endeavors to edify Cosmic Edict alright, he shall receive understanding. Unworkable knowledge is for the fool, Love is the beginning of Wisdom for it IS Love. Be not deceived, consciousness does not expand, it IS! Mind does not expand, it absorbs what ye feed into it, by this ye shall know unredeemed teachings as they tell you of expansion! Unfolding consciousness brings the soul into Truth. A beginner believes he can jump with both feet haphazardly into the whole, employs intellect and mortal reasoning rather than listening with the quiet soul. He manipulates psychic matter that in the end pulls him into the quagmire of self-undoing. Abstain from unlawful practice, Oh Pupil, the rushing into unknown dangers! Have flower seeds a blossom? Do they not unfold in due season? Does not sunshine and rain quicken the seed to grow into the flower before it wills to stretch its face toward the sun? And so it is, the unfolding soul must wait in patience, adhering to Him Who is the Way, Truth and Light, until Spirit pours out Its Essence and lifts the seeker step by step into Enlightenment. Man of earth is soul incarnate, must wait and weather every storm that shall be crowned with gladness, until the soul is well rooted in Eternal Matrix and personality finds perfection in the Divine Ego. Then no wall, no storm, no door can keep it bound to earth.

"Man need not be concerned with a hell, save the one he chooses to create for himself; but rather with the fate of soul in the final accounting that it can stand approved in merit to continue in the cycle of progress. Soul shall stand before the Inner Being to give just cause whether it has gained the right to continue or be neutralized by the Light into another form. Only few return to the Silent Cause to begin from the starting point. When ye stop running ye come into peace. In thy drudgery when ye pray and God keeps silent, It, the Formless It, trusts fully ye would work out thine own problems.

"Individual progression of the soul is recorded in the seed-record of the self, gauged by measures of soul-productivity, not quantity but quality of work, probed and counted in ways of conduct, motive, through testings and trials, all these! Meekness, fortitude, honesty, calculating the weight of results garnered by cause and effect, they are a part of the Judgment. But ye may come to Him, Who is the Way, Life and Light to every soul, in Him ye have final liberation, but without thine good consent He would do nothing!

"The Word ye speak peals out a sound that plays across the Eternal Harp of Consciousness. Each act, silent motive, hidden deed, for these ye are accountable. Let thy ways be worthy of presentation. Ye labored diligently through millions of existences, moved through portals of life and death perpetually, but now the time has come in that ye found the Way by which to become free if ye would consent. Let not thy utterings be flavored by conceit nor contempt, for verily I say, how does the body pay? Through the gills! Dwell not in guilt, rather endeavor to do well. Seek what IS, in the Eternal Now. Enter thy light-form to release the inner being into His Presence, it grants the key by which ye may overcome the lesser self.

"Ye know to love? Then seek not oblation of Spirit in religion, cult or like subsidies that please God by the way they perceive Him. There is no God man proclaims. The Formless One is beyond mortal comprehension and fantasy. The Essence of *IT* resides within each soul, each consciousness and in all of Nature it is *IT* omnipresent that is the only Lifegiver. He is the Light Bearer, the All Wise Presence. If man would look to *IT* in all creation, wars would cease to be and he would hallow the life in all. If man killeth any living thing he does not know God. It is the Melody of *IT* that healeth thee and makes the being every bit whole, none other is of value to thee, none other! The Lifestream links one to the other, the self ye are cannot be slain, it is birthless, deathless, forever, for it is energy and Energy is God.

"Corruptible as the flesh may be, soul is immortal. When the gales of hate and misqualified energy blow themselves out, man reaps the effects of his actions, pain brings him closer to the truth he is seeking. Outward search creates a deep chasm from here to Beyond that is the bottomless pit of self-undoing in which the beast of man dwells. For the sting of wrong action rebounds as man gloats from the throne of his corrupted kingdom and the oppressor becomes the oppressed. Man burneth in ignorance, persecutes the faithful who translate in effort to bring forth the Mandate of Truth that would untangle confusion. The wage of adulterated spirit-power and evil influencing is *REGRESSION!* Evil workers redeem their karmic debt in Astral Cosmos, sometimes another reimbodiment affords the chance of redemption as the body is deformed. There the light of Realization reminds him by the still small voice not to fall back into his former estate of thought or action. Oh, Beloved Seeker, man has not learned! Man seeks to preserve his standard of living, his dreams are nightmares as he hangs on to illusions that dissipate and precipitate into nothingness, as from nothing they ensued. His hidden inner life replays his conscious actions and there is no rest for the restless. He does not know that to live proper in the conscious self brings forth a change and betterment through the unconscious. The psyche is not a product of the self as it were, but the product of the unconscious life."

Cultivation of Spirit

"To those who read My Words I say, I speak not to humble thee nor to dampen the sweetness of spirit, but to prove the causation of ills that assail the soul of mankind. Cultivation of divine attributes are needful to the incarnate. Souls upon earth sow to decaying flesh to appease their pride, lusts and willfulness, what does it merit? Man believes in a God Who may or may not hear or heal him. Swashbuckling belief leads to violation of Cosmic Law and self-undoing. What ye call God lends no ear to vile utterings, for its mechanism of Light repels the shadow and ye feel the brunt! I pray the spirit shall be healed and the mind come into Its submission.

"The power to heal resides within every soul. To contemplate and experience Light brings forth the curative flow of its power. The curative Essence becomes active when ye believe It IS, thus ye experience Reality in unreality and Grace manifest. The humble soul needs but to nudge it and the Light of Mercy moves into action, to bless, to heal, to restore; for it is God, the Nameless Presence, all-pervading. The false teacher counsels ye shall not heal another lest ye would suffer his karma. Ye may heal in His Name if such is thy calling, for, the Power of Him Who is Truth, the Light, is the Healer who healeth whom He will and by such merit as the soul has earned. He alone lifts karma and none other than He. Since each must bear its own, none shall lift it, mayhaps, not even God! Ponder this.

"In cultivating spiritual being ye shall understand the proverb: 'With all thy getting, get understanding'— let thy thoughts, aspirations and prayerful intents be directed to the Formless One Who is the First Cause and Lifegiver of all. Ye experience Reality when ye realize Cosmos is thyself, turn the eyes of the soul of the Ocean of Love and Mercy out of which ye were born. Lay aside carnal belief that the Light may pull the being through the Open Door and Truth shall wash away the stain. Have trust in things unseen, for the Great Unseen is thy Reality and life. To know the Creator ye first must believe He IS. If man scoff the Reality of his own being, his passing shall affront him with a great truth, where another debt shall exact payment, for He that birthed thee is even thine own Self. Thus, at even-tide let thy prayer be for the Grace of Light, at daybreak thanking Him for Life.

"Erring indoctrinations lead to madness, abuse of power to regression. Royalty of old threw the faithful into dungeons of 'His Name's Sake' and superimposed their unrighteous precepts that defied all reason upon the humble soul. Those who teach eternal damnation do likewise, for 'the letter destroyeth, but the Spirit giveth Life.' They tell you to blot out the sixth sense, having never heard of the Seventh that moves consciousness into the God Worlds at will, that is the sacrament to spiritual freedom. Those ye know of that talk to spirits seldom believe they exist, yet they wield the ax of arrogance in abuse of holy power. I say, separate thyself from the chaff, that when ye see the Light or sparks of same, ye would know Its Eternal Fire is the Radiant Garment of His Holy Spirit that shall comfort thee.

"Having come apart from unholy alliances ye shall look into the heart of humanity to know the need, feel the pain and act by the empowerment of Spirit. And who is there to protest thy illumined state of being 'less they stood in the footless Self, endured pangs of regeneration and moved freely in the Lands of Spirit. Be not daunted in the supremacy of thine belief and practice! Wisdom blots out doubt and negation, Wisdom IS Love, the Love that lifts burdens, moods of anarchy serve the force of Asure. The myth of redemption fills the incarnate with uneasy curiosity, but once he lays the body aside, looks back to the form, what is left to be saved? The Gateway of Consciousness leads to the Open Court and freedom of soul, ascend to the Citadel and the dream of an earth life recedes back into illusion. Sciences grant insight but none can offer soul the reward of freedom, save soul itself enters the experience and knows!"

The Master fell silent. His light of Peace gave tranquility to my being. In retrospect of a past long gone, I felt the brush of madness from other existences and the yearning of yore to know the secret by which to become free. Somehow I felt newborn, coupled with flashes of past lives, chilling kaleidoscope visions of human evils rolled across the screen of my mind as the Master-Light regressed me to the point and days of witch hunts, torture racks and guillotines. My spirit felt faint as I beheld my various exits out of the earth world. A soft outpouring of warmth wrapped me into mists of white to pull me deeper into the sunshine of Spirit, a peace cleared away my thoughts as the Master continued:

Power of the Spirit

"Rose-Hanna, record! The personality cannot grasp the vastness of the indwelling Self nor perceive the enormity of its power. Do not study by reason but listen intently with the ears of soul. Cosmos is within, soul is Cosmos. Innate power is waiting to be used but Wisdom holds the reigns until the small self can show correct application of the first portion of life-energy entrusted in the beginning. The inner Self stands in the center of the individual universe, reaching into the vastness of inner and outer space, planes, worlds, and universes. As as evanscent star, soul harbors the finest frequencies of Spirit, magnetic qualities draw to the indweller all he desires, drive back all he rejects. Soul immersed in Sound and Light, aye, I say, the forces of nature shall do its bidding. Having conquered the barriers of personality and submitted the small self to the Higher Cause, incarnate consciousness realizes all is Spirit and Spirit is all. The mind becomes an effective tool of the soul, body and soul are the vehicles through which the God Force does Its own bidding, the abuse or misuse of power becomes unthinkable. The spiritual adept has risen above mind manipulation and lets go of mind itself to accomplish soul travel for now the Light directs the path that leads toward Masterhood Consciousness. His earthy losses or gains do not affect him with feelings of loss or pleasure, since he is now a dweller in all worlds and no longer slave to passions. His invisible shield of Light repels maligners who reap what they've sown, but beyond this he has no concern, more often it happens without his knowingness. The protective armor of the twice-born intensifies in frequency when the serving adept gives quitclaim to all personal, and in a sense Divine Power, the latter freely flows through him, reflects its essence back into the sea of Spiritual Consciousness.

"Thus, the Indweller has overcome the world, but the world does not understand his detachments that may earn him a reputation of being imbalanced, but detachments are his springboard to spiritual power in every way. I say, My Scribe, man is a being of glory, of light, a mystery discovered only by few. The countenance of the twice-born gives forth a luminous reflection that is felt by his brotherman, yea, these are refractions of the sun, stars, firmaments, and spheres that be! A wondrous light shines from his face, the cold Heat of the Presence flows unconsciously from him and the recipient of that Grace shall also ascend to this estate sometime, somewhere. The unredeemed individual is quick to scoff, to anger, filled with erring intents for he cannot reconcile to a life of peace since competition, confusion and warmonging keep the lesser self, the personality in check, drugged by its own temper. Thus he despises the Adept for unknown reasons, kills him off when he can, feeling the friction of unendurable finer forces. Not until the wayward turns to the Light can he slowly leave his ungodly estate and become at long last a noble soul.

"Salvation-self-elevation of consciousness accrues in all, mayhaps not until after many lifetimes. The free-willed self can accept or reject but the Light appears when ye least expect! Ye have come down to earth to perfect the self, to fulfill the Law, to aid the evolution of the whole, all else is folly. Ye can do without doing if ye choose, become the vessel, perfect and light-filled that lets the Power flow through as It wills!"

Thought Patterns

"I instruct thee in lessons of truth and morality that ye may grow wise and to acquaint thine True Self. In the light of regeneration I say ye shall think wisely, applying the goodly thought to every enterprise set before thee, for thy fervent thought is energy and creative power. Ye are father and mother to these that destroy or redeem. When ye think ye create! What creations stalk thy day? Right thoughts fortify thine household, the transmitter of thought energy forms into a manifested need. When ye think, ye pray, to pray in whining confusion withholds endearing results. When the mind is still, free of emotions, ye then think effectively. Man is what he thinks, shall he learn how to think right? Verily he would be unsnared from evil. Let thy thoughts be thoughtless, as flowers on a child's chaplet, consciousness is the tool. Let thy thoughts attain to no less but what is pleasing to Him, Who is the Truth and the Light. Thy thoughts leave a potent mark upon thy daily life, while it goes out and gathers unto itself like creations. What ye think ye become, what ye expel ye can in no wise retract nor all thine weeping shall wash it away.

"Keep mind harmless, morally clean, vice is no friend of creative thought. Speak not untruth, nor stretch it as ye endeavor to leapfrog at a better opportunity! Give not false promise for what ye promise to any being ye promise it to Him Who holds the Key and Cornucopia of every good. Keep harmless the elements that are that compound and consist in every living thing, for even the raindrop containeth worlds in the atom and through its sparkle ye can see into all eternity. Bear thou in mind, thy thoughts run out upon eternal seas and glide back to thee to manifest those things ye desired at the start. And if thy thoughts disappear into the substance of the Whole, ye, being a vital part of it, they must find thee again, even if after thousands of years. So I trust ye shall not think of what befalleth thee as an evil thing, but as thine own creation that cometh home to roost; and if perchance ye find a thing disturbeth thee, albeit ye dwell in the Life and Light of Love, ye have at long last found it within thine own creative power to think nobly and otherwise, I say, ye stumbled upon a great secret. As the Hidden One spoke to Job: 'Be thou perfect'—so he speaketh unto thee likewise this day: 'Be though perfect!' And ye shall see most beneficial results. The Wand of the Word points to self-perfection!

"Attain thy thoughts to that lofty heights were none can hinder, none offend and lose and loose the soul into the Life of thoughtless thought that would create the perfect manifestation of thine every noble and good desire in the world below and what ye decree shall be thy living blessing. Let thy perceptions be clear and deep, thy Holy Affection unchangeable that nothing can mar nor defeat nor dim its Glory and there shall be no sorrow or concern when ye embark.

"Rest now, My Scribe, this is all for this evening. I shall come again. Blessings and Grace rest upon each head."

In the Light of
Regeneration
I AM—Master—Y.—

Chapter Three

The Indwelling Presence

Weeks elapsed since my last dialogue with the Master, forlorn I sat under the out-branched umbrella of the Living Tree waiting....Its crown stretched high into the brilliant blue of Cosmic Skies and cast its shade across soft green meadows and whispering streams that rushed in silver-white effulgence along the footpath of God's Most Holy Mountain. Love's golden stillness permeated the air and a warm mystic breeze swept through the garden of consciousness, soothing my restless thoughts of where the Noble Master could be. Was this the end of all dictations? I wondered what kept Him.

Reminiscing, I addressed His unseen Presence: "Noble Counselor," I strained, "come now with Thy Teachings that Wisdom Light may quicken the soul of one and all. I pray, lift Thou the veil from my eyes to behold Thee more clearly, standing at the Gate, speak now!"

Silence prevailed. Then, a Golden-White Mist became my garment of Light. My hand and pen quivered fiercely as a warm, penetrating brightness streaked through inner chambers. The flushing heat of an electrical charge seared through my naked soul and out of the depth of an oscillating, shining mist spoke now a penetrating, clear Voice. My pen flew over the paper to record. Who it was I did not know; I feared to question. The Voice spoke out from my own deep self in the rumbling sound of clear words:

"Hear Ye! Ye who pen and ye who read My Sayings through the Scribe: I am the Indwelling Presence, the Lord of the soul, the Master of masters, that *I AM*! In your restless search of Me I permitted other masters to teach you in the Way, until in your frustrations, disgust and utter disillusionments you dropped all and drew unto Me only. I am your true Teacher, the Wayshower and nearer than hand and foot. I am the Way, the Door and Life of your own Light! Within you I am the Expresser of My Will, working through many vehicles to bring forth My Divine Idea, you ARE My Idea expressing as Myself. I am the living force in the soul of humanity, humanity is also my body. I am the Light of each soul, whether upon earth or in any other world or universe. There is none beside Me, worship none other! I am come forth from the center of the Ultimate, Absolute, the Life-Giver of Creations. I am in every teaching er' they be right or wrong, these serve Me to bring in My Truth that soul may learn through pain, tribulation, indecision, and testing. I am Wisdom, Love, Glory, and the Reality that flows through ever past, present and future of every tomorrow that is and is not; for ye live in eternity now, as even your every good realized is NOW. I am the Truth in all things.

"What you see in My son Jesus and you seek in every other avatar I have sent, is Myself but you may come to Me directly. You are the sons and daughters born of My immaculate Thought, you are gods who forget your noble heritage and you beg for scraps of bread and for the succor of the unrighteous. You are slaves to your habits and vice, slaves to your thoughts, entrapped by illusions. When you come to Me in self-willed obedience you shall learn to tell your mind what to think, your feelings what to feel and set your world into order that ye may worship the kernel rather than the husk! Then My Word shall be your scepter, a rod of strength by which you shall find the good measure of all things and overcome negations. Through you I am the Giver and manifestation of all good. You are Myself, the Word made flesh.

"Those through whom I teach the Way, are My personified Being, as I am also in you personified and I express through individualized consciousness that you may come into self-acknowledgment, Soul-Realization and God-Awareness. Obey therefore Cosmic Mandates, pray to receive My Peace to bring forth living truth to other souls and I shall open the Temple Doors to Widsom and they shall have life in the freedom of My Living Word that is food to every soul. It is well to speak of Love, but love as man proclaims is blind, it binds one to the other by the force of possessiveness and dominance, soul is earthbound until it willingly enters My Light and becomes free.

"Spiritual being is not one dimensional but experiences every dimension of the vast Beyond and beyond that. In the vastness of soul's own estate it may partake of My Reality and those activities that are, while still upon earth. Spirituality has no concern for unsettling issues, having experienced the balancing forces of Cosmos it remains detached from emotional issues. I say, come ye apart from turmoil of carnal living, rise above it in detached living, then, and only then shall nothing entice, infill and incite you more than God.

"To love one another is first command, in loving you shall find the peace that shifts every attention from troubling conditions to worthy endeavors. Spiritual being demands balance, calls out to subdue every destructive element and arrogant view of the personality and to release soul wholly into the Living Lifestream of Spirit where all is brought into regeneration and submission. When ears that hear harken to the Voice of My Indwelling Presence, the soul enters regeneration and finds true Love resting as a springtime blossom within the heart.

"Problems that assail humanity are reflections of your consciousness created to its self-undoing. What ye utter and think in silence ye must again reap, individually and collectively for even Global Karma affects one and all. Let actions and emotions remain pure, each motive be undefiled to create a strong, new foundation in the 'morrow and for all time to come; that the reality of the soul shall shine as a precious pearl from the eternal depth of the Ocean of Love and Mercy through the profundity of your purest, deepest, truest, affection ye call God.

"Truth points out salvation in the self-elevation of consciousness in which soul realizes what God is rather than what IT is supposed to be according to carnal concept and man's illusion. Soul is the immaculate Light manifest, the Thought of Creation made flesh. This singular I-ness has nothing to do with man's belief, religion, creed, altruism, or suffering, It remains impersonal; nor does it have anything to do with third and fourth dimensional teachings, the Life-Giving cannot be confined into the narrow compartments of mortal controversy.

"To draw into My Light that is thine own self, the Sound of My Word shall be understood, the plagues of selfhood eliminated. The Light-Experience sheds luminosity into soul's outer world and the personality is 'saved.' Transformation grants stability of mind. The realized soul knows it must live in lower world activity but heaven is its true home. Thus it becomes consistent in contemplating the Light and thereby freed from any earthbound tie, for it is now liberated, faithful to Eternal Creed and a bonafide citizen of Cosmos that adheres to the law of earth as well.

"Until soul consents to live in all worlds while still in the flesh, it remains bound to cycles of life and death and bound to the Wheel of sorrow, as well as the frights of death-illusions. Thusly it enters the interim sleep of twilight and lingers at the astral hearth to repeat its search for truth and God, whereas it may be realized at the present. Many make light of spiritual law, say there is no life after death until psychic entrapments and dangers prove otherwise. The Mandate: 'Thou shalt have no other gods before me' is ignored, eludes man's understanding, for it excludes the worship of every saint, savior, and savant and therefore leaves none other to be worshipped than the Formless One, Its Essence that manifests to the soul as Light in the Power of the Spirit of God that shall teach the soul all things. Man clings to idols and images he can touch whereby he rejects the Unseen that is his true reality. He fears to leave the house of clay since he has no conception of *what* God is, yet he lives because God Is, if God were not, he would cease to be without a hereafter!

"You speak of loving thy neighbor and other kindred souls, but if man does love his brother why does he slay, rob and deprive him of his right to think for himself? He incarcerates him for his spiritual allegiance and robs him of the human right to live in freedom. I say, the Law is unchangeable, is not changed by remorse or prayer, no saint shall step in to remove the suffering in effect to the cause until the law is fulfilled bit by bit. And ye seek forgiveness of God? Ye shall have it when ye have forgiven thyself!

"In thy learnings and endless groping I abide! I am the Indwelling Wayshower to the listening soul. All you are doing, I am doing with you, I express through you as life. As you dare and do the impossible, in Me is no mountain too big to climb. Only in Me can you recognize true power for the power you think you possess is Mine also which I permitted you to feel for the moment as you drew into My Nature. Church and cathedral are My outer expressions, you shall not find Me there for I am the Reality of your own Heart.

"Every condition in your life is My vehicle by which I move you into action as you go in search of Me. I am within the sound of your own breath but you perceive it not. I am the silent part of your love and hate, you find me glorified in your exaltation and in your sorrow and I am He, the Anointer of the Audible Word that healeth the broken in body and heart. But know, My Children, you are perfect in My Sight, there is no wrong in your True Self for I dwell in It and you in Me.

"Your steady inconsistencies are My opportune pleasure for they bring you unto Me in the end. Without me nothing is found, beside Me nothing exists. All of Eternity is in My Being. He who has found My Indwelling Presence does not turn back to dead issues, of what value are these? Time and time again ye lived in shallow cycles, eyes cast to the ground until the dust of it obscured the vision of Light. Awaken O Soul!

"When you turn from the duality of books and pseudo-masters, you shall find Me and the Life into which you cannot enter but through Me. Not until you drop all, forsake all, shall your ardent search of Me cease. I am the inborn Magnet that draws the ready soul through the crystal Light into His Heart. Come to Me without diplomas, props, belief, or crutch. Not until you forsake self-will and prideful adornments can you enter My Reality. And I say unto thee, seek ye not even My Presence for I am the Holy One within the soul and shall not remove myself. Throw away the broom by which you attempt to clear the mental closet, for the bristles of your mechanical techniques shall break and not bring forth the Light, neither does frivolous chanting nor ritualistic device usher in the freedom of spirit, lest ye would call on the Sacred Name of God!

"Learn what makes the day break, the bird sing and why! And you shall have come nearer My Truth and I say, lose yourself in discontinued thinking and My Light shall burst forth as the radiant sun of a bright, shining morning and draw you into My splendor to know you have found yourself in ME and I in you that the fatted calf shall be brought forth and Wine Eternal shall fortify the soul.

"Children of earth, practice the Reality of My Presence, come to me in your bridal garment for the table is set. Do not manipulate sacred energies, forcing procreative essence upward as does the fool, for such a one shall suffer debilitation. Only in

My Nature can soul enter the Mystical, Conscious Union with God. I have given to man and woman the pleasures of loving to be expressed in a bond of holy union such is My Law to man upon earth; that in sacred giving of one to the other love shall be sanctified that the seed of the First Adam spring forth. In faithful simplicity of loving, the seed of man shall not be cast to the ground of degeneration. In the harmony of giving and receiving you shall bring forth the fruits of love, life, wisdom, and charity, for these are My Attributes.

"Scribe, you ask about celibate living, balance must be and creative energy directed into channels of work, a task, servitude and spiritual creativity as it were. To abstain from physical union is not harmful as scholars determine. In search of My Reality a mate is denied to some for a time, that in mystical celibacy the being would abstain from physical pleasures and soul-energies be fortified by empowerments of Spirit, to regenerate and strengthen the forces that be, that soul would remain undepleted and cicumvent for a mission. I here speak to serving consciousness rather then to average man.

"In your aloneness turn to the immortal self, I am the Perfect One you seek, the true mate of every soul. When the feminine/masculine aspect becomes neuter, *I AM*. Remain in Light that the Sound shall bear you up to give account of what IS in the Realities of Cosmos, at this time thy way of isolation is needful.

"The profanity and idolatry of self-manipulation brings demise upon the offender, for the seed is holy and shall not be cast to the ground. He who seeks sexual lust as his ultimate fulfillment, behold, a Keeper stands at every Gate. Material comforts are the God of the unrealized but more, because underneath all surface appearances gnaws the subconscious hunger, the yearning for truth. Co-creative power is the Mystery of Life revealed when the soul gives detached, impersonal Love to life, then creative energies rise naturally upward by the cold heat of Spiritual Fires that give birth to the Impersonal I, that *I AM*, through the personal self.

"The error of mockery, of idolatry and lust bring forth warmonging and self-destruction. My Love gives Peace, satisfaction to the heart, my Spirit flows through the vessel's free will, without your consent I would do nothing. In creativeness and destruction, I am there. My Force enables the soul to rise above its negations, quickened by the Wine of Life and Living Bread it can go out and quicken other souls and it shall know no other Will but

Mine. When the personality feels bound to earth by conditions, it is because the finer part of the self is yet unrealized. Be patient with yourself, be patient! If ye say ye love Me, behold what ye despise, aye, I am in all of these and all is within you!

"Until My Reality is recognized within you and awakened, you remain in the humble estate and in your hypocritical displays of Love you are the thief claiming My Glory for himself! For mark ye well, I am in the poor in heart as I am within you, I am in the lonely rich, neither the infant's smile nor the pain of the dying can hide My Reality, for THAT I AM. Learn to love yourself, loving Me and you shall bring under control and to kneel the animal before the manger of the Light and you shall be the gate-keeper and watcher over your self-indulgent flesh.

"Be at Peace, *I ABIDE*, Go now, ponder My Sayings...!"

I AM
—The Indwelling Presence—

So I pondered the Words of the Voice that spoke out from the deep Wells of Light and asked it would help us conquer the unfinished self and to use what it could for service. All became silent, save the chirping of song birds near the window. I felt a trailing glow of Love, renewed courage and the willingness to bring my scattered ideas under one roof to release them to Spirit. The Voice of the Indweller enabled me to affirm, that no matter how fierce the winds of destiny blew across life's path, a part of me could stand unmoved and forge onward, clasping the Hand of our silent, Omnipresent Partner, The Light.

More dialogues and discourses followed. At times the Magnificent One, the Master-Light, would lift me upon sunlit greens in Cosmic Dimensions that became memorable events.

A Journey Within—The Pink Crystal Chalice

"And I took it, and drank; and when I had drunk of it, my heart uttered understanding, and wisdom grew in my breast, for my spirit strengthened my memory. Then opened I my mouth, and behold, he reached me a cup, which was full as it were with water, but the color of it was like fire." (Apocrypha 14:39-40)

Again, days passed, no sign nor word from the Master, save lost, wandering entities that I directed into Light without conversation. I sat beneath the altar-lights in my chapel keeping pen and pad at hand, just in case....

Now candle lights flickered strongly, soft heavenly effulgence swept through the twilight of my humble habitation, a swirling, moving energy interrupted the reviewing of former messages I held on my lap and a great force gently carried me inward. I felt a dim, pulsating fog that lay across Etheric Pathways, sensed a heaviness all around, my earthly pen had dropped from my hand.

"Where am I?" I questioned silently, when a blinding Light soared towards me, it bore me up as on wings of an eagle. As scooped up by a rushing wind my footless spirit lifted along a winding path into etheric gardens, scents of rose, jasmine and lotus mixed with breath of sweet lilac swished around my head, a glorious sight that wonderland of the Gods!

Velvet carpets of soft flowing greens stretched into Cosmic Highlands, the chirping of song birds enhanced lustrous golden pathways that led to a great body of living waters, smooth and still. A starlit conopy reflected its image from the deep of the clear waters, silvery light-threads rayed back up to the firmament. I carried along white ocean sands, soul wrapped in nature's living wonders. Awe-entranced I found myself standing before a wishing-well. Its colorfully arrayed gems surpassed in beauty all imagination. So I dropped my fondest hopes into its clear, bottomless depth, but in dismay I saw it vanish from sight.

A feeling of profound aloneness sought to pull me into its negative web. My mental plea rang out: "Saints, deliver me, Master, where are you?" This was not the sunlit path of Love I knew, but the treacherous realm of Maya's beautiful illusions. The word 'Halmaya' echoed through me. I felt entrapped by my venture as darkness drew all about. Now my Guardian of many journeys stepped out of the mist that obscured Him from sight. His soulful eyes shone into my core with compassion, restoring immediate peace. He sternly spoke:

"Rose-Hanna, be not entranced by illusions that have no heart and trap soul. The ethers of Maya like those upon earth dissolve all substance not eternal. Soul must strip away idolatry and superficial want, for even here all is cosmic tinsel! Rest now, my pupil, drink of this cup!"

I reached for the clear crystal chalice filled with rosy pink nectar and drunk it to the bottom. New life flowed through all my being, my senses became most clear. I realized that need and want were unrelated and that to release soul into the Master-Light would grant answers and the key to unlock every portal in search of God.

The Key To Heaven

Rosy-pink elixir ran rejuvenation through my being, all around me was crystal-clear to my sharpened senses. Evening dew lay across the rose-scented pathways of Etheria, the warm mystic breeze carried in the echo of Golden Crescendos from afar. Now heavenly sights gave way to an aura of purple deep. A sick feeling reeled through me as I spun out of my light-body into the High Reaches of true God-Worlds, through mists of Mystic Twilight into golden spheres of chiffon splendor. Except for being able to know and see I knew no other sensations or feeling. My naked being emerged into Eternal Light, my knowingness pierced through the ecstasy: would I now release my individuality and remain forever in this rolling splendor of Love and Mercy? I couldn't tell. Insurging inspiration embraced me from every direction and in true God-Realization I did consent to become whatever was to be, even if but a sparkling drop of joy in this living effulgence. Strangely though, I felt it to be a part of me. Beyond all worlds of thought I was all-knowing energy immersed in rapturous Sound and Light, yet soundless stillness. Protective Love reigned all about. A soft pressure from an unseen force, and at a speed much faster than light I traversed back into other dimensions of cosmic life. A slow motion brought me to face a massive portal of a Temple-Door. Its gold studded wings bore an inscription I could not discern.

My Noble Traveler in White stood beside me, His auric mantle pured forth discharging rays of colorful light, still magnifying the Mystic Light of Golden Ethers. It shone in the brillance of the sun, obscuring His statuesque form for moments. Then all turned again to endurable brightness and the Master handed me a key. As I felt its weight it vanished, so did the portal, we had been transported to lower dimensions; but as I looked, the small golden key lay in my hand and the Venerable Counselor spoke:

"Rose-Hanna, use this key wisely. In love it shall open many doors for the self and others. In hours of healing it shall summon the forces of Light and you shall behold the natural wonders of God manifest. As you decree so shall it be upon earth as it is in heaven." I looked in astonishment, why me? The Master knew my thoughts and handed me a scroll, it read: "I now give unto thee the key of Love, whatsoever ye grant shall be granted, whatever ye shall bind shall be bound, bind not a living thing!" And so it came to pass as I decreed it. So I lay the golden key upon the altar of my heart to use, cherish and hold sacred.

By a soft touch of His Light the Master moved me back into earth vibrations, again I consciously picked up my pen to record the Sayings of my Exalted Instructor that still softly resounded through upper chambers:

"Beloved Scribe, immerse soul into Sound and Light, yeah, ride upon its waves into all Eternity, fear not the tempest it shall not harm. What you decree shall be. Soul must enter the baptismal Fires of Holy Spirit Power to enter again the Heart of the Eternal at journey's end, Who was, is, and ever shall be. Therein lies the Reality of the Kingdoms of Heaven. Only in your light-form can Reality be entered, all else is naught. Only in soul-form pure and clean can consciousness return home into the Ocean of Love and Mercy that birthed it.

"Each must find courage to break through the Gate, there is no other Door. When soul submits to regeneration, slow and sure as it may be, the Life-Giver shall grant freedom and give the Love to use, heal and redeem.

"Beloved earth-brethen, I would ye might live in detachment, er' ye might fall pray to negations of the world at large. When ye feel the weight of the world, come ye apart and sup with Me. Hold tightly the key of spiritual gold and ye who heard my Word, know, *I ABIDE*!

"Rest now, Beloved, what was experienced write into a book. I shall come again. My Blessings I grant, abundant Grace rest upon one and all——"

—Master—Y.—

Many other journeys to Cosmic Highlands followed, so did appear other Celestial Teachers to bring Their Truth, Holy Counsel, Dialogues and Dispensations in dictations that shall now be given to my thoughtful Reader in succession; to warm the heart in regeneration, to lift the soul to Love's Sacred Worlds and grant to all the Holy Succor found in the Precepts of Sound and Eternal Light.

Chapter Four

Precepts in Regeneration

Behold, I send an Angel before thee to keep thee in the way, and to bring thee into the place which I have prepared." (Exodus 23:20)

Instructions from Divine Intelligences are stronghold to every soul. The selfless service of God's Shining Host is untiring, unfailing, the Great Unseen our true Reality. Silent Helpers guide willing souls through portals of Initiation into spiritual freedom. Our desired answers may not always come through dictations, but often in ways of new-found strength, new directives, renewed health, profound uplifting, that we may realize God's Indwelling Nearness and Benediction.

Silent Servers attend souls upon earth and each has a Guardian before the Throne of God, but they do not remove needful testings and the birthpangs of regeneration. Their Holy Influence and Intercession softens the blasts of life's storm. They renew within us a great faith in ourselves and God, reinforce our fortitude, the steadfastness in spiritual practices. Pray without ceasing becomes the motto, each rightful thought a prayer—that positive energy may turn sorrow into the smile of a brand new life, always under the guiding Forces of God.

Dictations from a Being of Light

During talks with the Spiritual Master, He said if we would grasp the meaning of the true Genesis that began long before Adam and Eve, we could go on to continue in Higher Dimensions, having at long last rediscovered our innate relationship to God. I've met the Master *ARAM YADAH* on Inner Planes during my out-of-body journeys. He stands tall, statuesque, in the shining glory of godly attire. Pearly white teeth under well-formed lips,

His soulful dark eyes shone deeply into my heart, nothing escapes Him. Master *ARAM YADAH* holds an honored post in Spiritual Hierarchy: He is a Silent Traveler with many functions. He also teaches the precepts of regeneration that aid soul-progression upon earth. We've frequented the spiritual world of Venus together, where I attended many of His lectures and later I channeled some of His teachings for the children upon earth, penned them as best as I perceived His Words. Excerpts of a dictation are here given:

"Greetings from Cosmos, Greetings from Hierarchy. *I AM* come to comfort, *I AM* standing in the Arch Light of the portals of thy consciousness to say: the difficult days are nearing a close when the student of truth adheres and obeys Inner Counsel in the precepts of regeneration. Indeed, ye have endured such as ye experienced pain in body and mind, aye, in thy greater force fields. Regeneration must be! Oh, My Beloved, that ye would abstain from self-willfulness, for fear follows pain, fear is not of God.

"Ye fall prey to the tempest, have felt the whiplash rebounding. The Flame of Light dances before the inner sight in loving enticement with a mission of good will for all, a destiny well revealed that ye may say in the end: how glorious, to this shall I treat, unto this noble goal I shall give my allegiance, yeah, let it be to the Spiritual Government of the King and not to a self-ruled life!

"And then horizons beckon clear, thy life, thy work take on new purpose and thy feet tread along a better path than ye followed of yore; for, I say, in the Christ, the Light-Consciousness by Whom ye receive the benediction ye shall be made every wit whole! For the Son of Light shall aid, direct and give Holy Succor.

"We, Servants of the Lords of Karma, sit in the High Courts of Cosmic Hierarchy of Light, grant goodly gifts and well justified burdens to souls, that ye may grow strong through what ye endure for thine own sake in purification. Then the robe ye spun through loving giving, and thy works rendered unto God shall be spotless. A noble attire indeed, the Christ-Bride shall wear to meet the Groom and receive total liberation in holy wedlock.

"Ye look for magic potions that would lift consciousness spontaneously to supreme heights, not so, I say, the Way *IS*, well earned must it be. Apply thine ear to Wisdom and ye shall come to know Love in its entirety, for Wisdom is Love, thus thy cup of happiness shall be full to running over. I speak to the weeping heart this day, that strength and peace might be restored, that the bonds of Bahl be shattered and the cords of ignorance snapped forever. It is not Divine Will that any soul should suffer, suffering is self-induced.

"If man would come to know himself, he would know God, the Formless One, the Life-Giver, Who is the *IT*, untouchable, ever-present! He is all things, everyone, even the malefic thing of man's own doing that brings pain, deformation of sorts and sorrow instead of reformation. What then is suffering? Why sickness? It is the rotating, churning action felt by the individual, as the Immaculate, Indwelling Self attempts to redeem him. God neither judges, nor destroys. Being the inborn self it simply frees its deadlock from the dross, thus leaves man to his own undoing, look around, Scribe, see what is being undone!! Sickness assails those who live in error, to some, unfortunately sickness is the teacher, it tends to humble in many ways. Often it is a culmination of breaking spiritual law throughout many existences, not necessarily errors of the present, that must be rectified. No one can die to redeem these, but the carnal self. Repentance means not to repeat the same error, think upon these words. The error of omissions is equal to the error of commission by intent. But the individual must not dwell on what was, but rather upon what IS—for ye are the sum total of soul-energy that moved through many lifetimes, the parent of thy misdeeds, misqualification of evergy and what ye sow ye reap. Harken to the Voice of Spirit, the still small voice, it speaketh aloud to those who have ears. Illness is the redeeming purgation, whether from within or the effect of environs, nothing, nothing can happen to a soul less it was earned.

"Man's terrible anger, selfishness, greed, pride, and vice, the karmic effects of self-willed pain grind the chaff to dust and the tares are consumed by the Light until the day when fear and avarice shall crawl back into the abyss of darkness and sickness shall cease to be. Then, at one glorious moment the etherealized self ascends, not in parts, but in wholeness of being as was exemplified by the Christ.

"Man seeketh the Christ forever, I say, he is the Christ embodied, who came into the first Adam and into every other man since him, to know this is to know thyself. This is the Law the man Jesus came to fulfill, that ye would know thyself and love one another. I say, walk ye in the indentations of His Example, for herein lies thy victory, thy triumphs are found in true precepts of regeneration. Ye must flow with the rhythms of harmonious life, then the Light shall blot out the shadow, but light cannot enter a house where shades of superstition are drawn tight as a harness, it never imposes, for: 'without thy mind He would do nothing.'

"Within thy very self lies the power to overcome the world, thy innate world, by which ye may lift the burden of the Whole. Ye are the Hand of God subduing the earth, the self, ye are the Will of God in action, ye are Christs, every one, called by many names.

"Ye cry for a savior, He is Omnipresent. Ye can meet Him Face to face when ye enter the Spirit of Love and behold Him in His Radiant Form. Be not deceived, many there be that would shout: I am HE! Be not deceived, none upon earth in the present era hold Saviorship, but one—that is the Inner Master, the Holy Spirit. For, the Mandate ever declares: 'Thou shalt have no other gods before Him!' And when ye meet a true Master in the flesh, ye shall find him perfect, without vice, without the desire of the flesh, wedded to God-Spirit. For they do not marry, their joy is full in God. Earth Masters are teachers of the Way, never saviors. And I admonish in counsel: worship ye none other than the Inner Being, all else is folly. A true Master incarnate, teaches not out of books, nor does he quote, he teaches the Way out of experience in the Higher Life. Follow Him who is the Light and the Way, for His Masterhood Consciousness was blameless.

"For in Him, ye shall enter the audible Sound of Life, the Holy Shabd. The audible lifestream is life itself, it flows through every action, and becomes the glorious melody upon which ye may travel into the sunlit Cosmos and become free.

"One claiming to be master of earth never takes donations, he must earn his own living and shares of that. A true master never imposes, materially or astrally. Beloved, be not deceived, 'God is not mocked.'

"Rama, Tao, Buddha, Osiris, Jesus, and other world saviors before Him carried the Flame of truth into the darkness of man, but darkness perceived it not. I gaze into hearts to aid, but their will is weak. Many step unto the ramparts of regeneration, grow disgruntled and flitter back as the moth to the light into worldy tinsel, to re-enter another form of clay, sometime, somewhere in their quest for spiritual freedom. Some glimpse God-Reality say it is folly, a second glimpse, they call it well, yet another and soul wants to jump head over heels into the Cosmic Ocean but suffers the consequence of such irrational action. Slow, sure and sane the approach must be, heaven is not taken by storm. When soul is ready, the Master appears. The struggle between light and darkness persists, but victory is won for the Living Guardian assists.

"In nature's way of patience, of ease, eternal secrets are revealed and following Her precepts ye shall not lose one tittle of thy well earned lot. If soul would be still, observe nature, it is the road-sign to Eternal Being. When soul observes, so does the Eternal Watcher."

The Master bade my heart peace, for moments all fell silent, only the old clock on the wall kept ticking away, the deep gong snapped me out of tranquility but soon again the Golden White Mist appeared on Inner Horizons and the Master ARAM YADAH continued:

The Monad and Over Soul

"What ye absorb of divine teachings is not learning, but a realization of inflowing Divine Love that bestows unfoldment. Each takes out of a teaching its own and there are many levels/states of consciouness to which the being aspired. Knowledge is Light, Wisdom is Love, the Love souls incarnate seek. Love is never an outer expression, save it flows out in benediction to all. Unfoldment is soul's unique experience, has nothing in common with ritual, belief or creed. God-Unfoldment, God-Realization in state of total awareness leads to the fulfillment of every noble aspiration, the highest to which souls upon earth can aspire. Wisdom/Love lifts consciousness from degeneration into the Audible Lifestream of regeneration, into the Sound, the Light and a Cosmos teeming with Life. Thus ye overcome death as did the saints, whereby all passions of the flesh are layed to rest.

"Where there was anger, ye find meekness and forgiveness,

"Where there was greed, ye found contentment,

"Where there was attachment, you found detachment from all things,

"Where there was pride, ye live in humiliy
"Where there was lust, a newly discovered chastity,
"Where there was impatience, there is loving kindness
"Where there was vice, there is virtue. There is more!

"In the realization of the precepts of regeneration ye moved into higher levels of consciousness, not mind—but Spirit, for mind is the tool of Soul, as soul is the instrument of Spirit. The all-seeing Watcher, Spirit, never sleeps. I say, the monad of atma-buddhic energy linked to he monad of form is the Guardian Light that safeguards every soul. It registers its every encounter in its sojourns through any world, that ye experience from life to life, age to age. Through windows of the conscious form soul reads, absorbs, so incorporating the energy of every happening into its seed-filament.

"While the lesser light sleeps, the Over-Light remains alert. Not only registering the energy from the waking personality, but it also records that of the dreamstate and subconscious reactions to same, as soul continually works out its karmic patterns. When soul wanders off into the frolicking of its outer world, forgets its causation for being upon earth, the Master counsels in its dreamstate, which the waking consciousness clearly recalls. The Over-Light is keeper of its lesser soul-light, the helper in distress. Never shall harm overtake its lesser part without its own consent. Soul is never lost, 'less it insists on demoralizing actions, degradation of spirit, or determines to sink into the drags of carnality. Even though it is given innumerable opportunities before the day of final reckoning; then, if change is not evident, it simply seeps back into the Mother-Light of its Father/Creator where soul's divine aspect enters a different form altogether to start anew, just as much as the redeemed consciousness by free will and choice may re-enter the Ocean of Love and Mercy to enjoy bliss Infinitum, or take a post in spiritual government as co-creator with God. Each has free will and choice. Or, to lay down its ego, merging totally and fully aware into Love is its own choice. Embodied consciousness must thrive to rise above its lower sense world lests it prolongs its stay in realms of matter. But what is matter?"

The Subject of Matter

"Beloved of God, we shall clear up a matter greatly misunderstood. Matter is not worthless, useless conglamoration, for to a degree it is crystallized spirit. Spirit and matter are only found as duality to the beholder, in that they are of opposite polarity, yet one belongs to the other. When matter is etherealized we have a fine spiritual substance, as the Master demonstrated at the moment of His transfiguration, the Ascension.

"Matter being a negative ray of spirit is the outer vehicle of the radiant soul ye are. Yet an illusion that fades back into its natural state, spirit, and turns into the dust, the salt of the earth enveloped by the nature or soil of the physical/material world, until the day when purified, etherealized atoms ascend as a whole. All experiences taking place in and within outer matter serve Divine purpose. Decomposition of the body has been thine own choice, ye can alter that estate by living a karmaless life. Ye cannot violate nature in *ANY* form and expect to redeem the self wholly!

"The aware soul, contemplating spiritualization knows the nature world creates and decomposes, in effort to redeem itself the individual begins to listen to the sounds of inner worlds, perceives Divine Inflection that entice the inner self to draw into alignment with the Monad of Spirit; that the lesser individuality would cease to be governed by outer circumstances, but rather by spiritual government; thus it acquires the art to scale the higher heights of beingness and is on its way to self-redemption. The finer the atunement to the Over-Light the greater its radiance diffusing the outer form that is visible to the eye and is felt as heat by other persons. Here we see the correlation of matter and spirit. The carriages, light-bodies connecting to the radiant soul, are composed of celestial atoms. Even though a mind filled with malice or steeped in materialism can obscure the Light, it remains ever-present, for it is soul's very life.

"When pondering the light-forms ye experience them as various shuttles that serve in shifting consciousness to corresponding dimensions of Higher Life activities, until the shining self consents to drop all sheath and enters the Ocean of Love and Mercy. Yet, the individual picks up each vehicle on its descent into the physical, material world. While soul leaves its earthly confines, the Master-Light watches the form, there is no danger if ye follow Him who is the Way and the Light by which ye see. Magnificent ye are! The God-Man is governed by the Grand Monad, the first two comprise the soul. And I say, what is there in all of life, in man or otherwise that has not sprung forth from Divine Love, mercy and Wisdom? In that, ye see, man is not self-created, is he not divine? God is, ye are and ye are because He IS! Ponder my sayings. Ye are not adopted, not a foundling, ye are *HIS*, until the day ye can fully identify with what God is and say: *I AM THAT*!"

A Discourse on Spiritual Garments

"When the incarnate personality renounces every lesser attribute it begins to make conscious use of immortal powers. It recaptures the art by which it may move freely through the God-Worlds to experience what truly IS. The greater its refinement, the better it can endure celestial ethers and the higher or farther it can go. Yet, at one point it does not go anywhere, it knows and experiences what IS! For verily I say, it takes its garments off and puts them back on as the clothing of its outer form. Thus it conquered matter, time, space, and death, experiencing eternal beingness outside of the flesh, that heretofore hindered and bound. Taking flight, the Monadic Flame periodically rises to a brilliance that shineth as a beacon light to soul's inner and outer worlds. It is the Inner Being, the True Self, the Glory! It stands like a candle in the midst of darkness. It shineth as a diamond of many facets, does as it pleases to fulfill Divine Intent in its sojourn through earth, aye, I say and far beyond realms of matter! It is no longer bound by matter, time or space in any form. It feedeth on the fuel of every holy thought and leaves the house of clay on its own velocity, while it revitalizes body and mind, the body ceases to hold it back. During its daily contemplations, the individuality experiences the glory of its brightly shining self.

"My Scribe, body, mind, soul are thusly in God-Harmony, the Indweller sings a happy tune, strengthens the fabric of its garments that the eagle may soar high, in triumphant cry as it loosens the shining atoms from the dense form, gathering up new ones into the wings of glory.

"I say unto all, the hour cometh that ye shall no longer pant in uncertainty, but experience the Life that is to the full, ye shall hear the Clarion Call of Freedom!

"Earthly cosmos giveth instruction and a torment profitable

to the seeker—and if mayhaps ye would forsake they dreads and terrible fears, and rather engage in the pleasures of spirit, ye shall know, being free at last, freedom is not as ye know it to be upon earth, for, the ways of world government bind, persecute and say ye are free when ye are otherwise. Beloved earth-brethen, ye must discern between the Voice of God and that of the great lie, that keeps souls upon Terrra in infernal bondage, her voice speaketh through evil workers and the clergy of the silent grave, aye, I say, of death of spirit, of soul, thine own imperishable self. But ye shall know truth, for death is but the taking on of a better cloak, as a bridal garment for a Great Celebration. And ye shall see the golden moment when thy life and love remaineth with thee and ye shall feel the freedom I bring unto thee this day."

Cast Off the Old

"The God-Man is not as man perceives Him. How can eyes webbed with envy, deceit, aye, fornication perceive the Teacher? Can some see his radiant form? I say he cannot. Neither do the spiritually deaf hear the melody that plays across the strings of the twice-born, nor do they perceive the Golden Tongues of Spirit. Cast off the garments of evil that vex thy spirit, follow not the piper into the nets of corruption, I say unto all, treat not with soothsayers that would rob the soul of its innate right to think free, act free and to freely express thy findings of Truth, of Cosmos! If ye need a life-raft, the judgment call of pulpiteers shall not supply it! Be not mesmerized by what appears or appeals like a new revelation but adhere the personality to the tried and true that would bring the soul into His Realization and an awakening without compare. Tread softly, speak kindly, keep the self harmless in all manner of things. And look not at the wondrous results of given energy as thy special gift but as the part of Him that came into thine well earned unfoldment. Fear not, O Children, fear not anything at all, for He speedily delivereth from the corruptor.

"Ye are born of Majesty, of the Immaculate Flame, can ye be less than That, that sired thee? Ye are lesser Gods until ye consent and content to rise to thy Father's Occasion in Perfection. Holy Blood courses through thy veins, lest ye pollute it, defile it, become laggards, drunkards, harlots, and the 'salt would lose its savor.' Nay, I would not offend thee, merely guide thee to cast off the old in heavenly precepts of regeneration to redeem the unfinished self.

"Thy every good shall be given, if ye would fasten the eyes of soul upon Him that watches over thee as over the sparrow. He healeth the broken wing and broken in heart, and the sparrow soars high, thinkest itself the eagle! Its song of praise resounds sweet melody upon Eternal Seas. Likewise ye are cared for, why doubt? Ye pray consistently: 'in earth as it is in heaven'—would help be only Above and denied thee upon earth? I say not! Ponder these Words. Ye receive as ye can conceive, what doest the heart conceive?

"I leave unto thee a peace that endureth forever, I leave with thee a blessing and trust thine faith to be strong, courage to carry thee onward, that thy cup of Love be offered to Him only, Whose Light ye carry forever in thine heart.

"The Light waiteth to teach thee—

"In Grace I came, In Grace I remain—

IN THE PRECEPTS OF REGENERATION
I AM
—ARAM YADAH—

A Message From the Mystical Brotherhood

"Greetings, Beloved of the Light;

"We come to you in the Light of Truth, in the Power of the Force that aids transmutation of error and refinement of energy upon earth. What is error? if not rampant energy scattered in erring directions. Right thought, right action, right speech, lovingkindness, these loom the way to happiness in the material universe. Offer thy good deeds, thy selfless service to Him Who is Supreme, that in Him ye may rise above the creations of karma, of pain, of sorrow. And karma shall have no effect on thee, death shall lose its sting, for ye shall know what IS and be free. Every test, task, and yearning, offer to Him Who is Perfection, in His Name. Fix thy thoughts, love and devotion on the Master of Masters, His Holy Breath, the Spirit and Its Eyes shall guard thee as the apple of the eye. For the Will of Him is the Will of the Father and ye shall become His Will in action, rich in Love and that Love shall lift thee through the White Mist into Lands of reality and joy, light and cosmic melody; and ye shall be fully conscious in communication with Cosmic Life.

"We, thy Elder Brothers, show the Way to Archaic Truth that underlies all religions and beliefs, it gives a clear insight on matters concerning regeneration, life, death, and the Immortal Spirit. Thy faithful earth brothers deem heaven, hell, purgatory, and the grave to be the ultimate destiny of all. Limited belief takes a path of resistance, believing in luck rather than Grace, but the true seeker of mystical life garners Divine Understanding and a state of spiritual awareness that is attained through active introversion, active contemplation, non-resistance, detachment, and a sensible placidity that belongs to Higher Consciousness. He enters a path of experience, no longer following a system of belief, for, to experience is to know! This way of beingness acknowledges the Nature of God to be rooted in every true spiritual experience, and knows the embodiment of God to be in every living thing upon earth and throughout all Cosmos, universes upon universes, worlds without end.

"Communications with Spiritual Teachers, Angels, Saints, Silent Travelers, Guardians are hallowed, yet not extraordinary, when ye come apart from the clamor of wordly excitement, ritualism, ceremony, and carnal activities to give ear to the Counseling Voice.

"Once the start is made and ye set time apart each day to attune the self to spiritual Guidance, ye found a connection that is reinforced more and more by thy willingness to listen in obeyance to what is given and to record same. The Voice of Love, of Truth, never loses luster, rather it increases in clarity and momentum as time moves on. It is important to recognize Creative Love, the Sound, for when it speaketh to one, it honors, nudges all! At times ye may tremble when the gentle, stern Power softly electrifies, tenses thy vessel to perceive more clearly the dictation; for inner adjustments and conditions must be met, only then shall ye perceive and hear on pure levels in a more lofty height and state of awareness to receive the Master's Word. That Sound, that Word, accompanied by luminosities of Light rejuvenates the self, clears perception as nothing else can, for this is 'the true light which lighteth every man coming into the world' that, in the words of Paul ye may exclaim: 'we testify to that which we have seen [heard] and bear witness to that which we know' and this, Beloved of the light, becomes thy living Truth.

For within thine own self He has promised to meet thee, to speak with thee face to face and only the pure heart and cleansed mind can behold Him clothed in His radiant Light, and ye shall hear Him repeat: 'the work that I do, ye shall do also.' For, 'when ye seek, ye find' and thy Inner Portals shall open, for such reads the Law.

"Thoughts from books and various teachings are well for the young student, but the day cometh when ye see the Law reserved for thee a teaching in secret that is thine, and thine alone as ye intently listen to Him, the It, that is the Way, the Light and the Life. For He holds the Nectar that quickens the heart, the soul, and the silent Word by which ye are made perfect and every wit whole. And ye shall let go off what was to know what truly IS and letting go of dead-wood teachings ye then live in the Eternal *NOW*, and the chains of the past have dissolved; a great realization of God may now enter the being. What matters it what, who or where ye lived before? It is past, lessons learned, needful growth acquired, ponder not the past but attain thy Love and thoughts to the hour, nor take thought of tomorrow, it is always—now.

"*ALL* good, all loveliness embues the Soul of mankind, it is thy own and shall find thee again and again; that thy cup shall be heaped up to running over, unless ye choose to let it be drained dry and weep into it to fill it back up! Beloved of the Light, no profit accrues from negations!

"Ye say thy tenth is given to orders claiming Christ is knocking at the door of the heart for contributions? We say: the King *IS* the Source of all Bounty, He has no need to wrest from you a token! Learn to unlearn! That ye realize the gigantic storehouse rests within thy self, ye hold the key to every bounty! Let thy sharing come forth in quiet giving to bear fruit, give without thought or remembrance and today's lack shall be tomorrow's Bounty.

"Ye came into our teachings not by choice, but by Grace. The very fact that ears are unstopped to listen permits, invites us to speak. And we say, 'with all thy getting, get understanding' thus ye shall define between need and want. And when need arises and a tear mists the eye, we say, God is in all of these, all-expressing, ever-embracing, uplifting at that very hour. Be not centered in the self, but lose that self in thy Other Selves until every cell and atom giving up to God express wholly in Him. For in giving up shall be harmony, prosperity and peace."

The Robe

"Thy garments of soul are as fashionable robes, a kingly attire. Thy thoughts interlace, changing colors and frequencies according to *WHAT* ye project into the forcefield, weave into its fabric. The Robe that grows in effulgence is the chariot by which ye leave the density of matter behind, it is a lamp unto thy feet. It gains in invisible and visible splendor, strength and Force by the degree of dedication, worshipfulness, love, charity, and honesty of thought and action by which ye infuse thy garment of ascension. From our Worlds we behold the colors of many Robes, some red with anger and other dense coloration that for a time obscure the Light. Other garments shine in soft indigo fading into the purity of White Light which their senses magnified.

"With thy every thought the shuttle flies, weaving the Robe ye shall wear in the 'morrow until the pure kernel of spirit returns to its home, to the Ocean of Love and Mercy. Beloved earth-brethen, ye write the book of life by innate energy upon the finest atom of the seed-self by every thought, every action. We trust thy flawless texts shall stand well approved by the Reviewer. Whether in seat of high courts or in common place, thine chosen work is part of time self-identification and a *MINISTRY* by which ye benefit the whole. In lieu of it, what seemeth unpalatable labor, unpleasing or even difficult would rather become a pleasurable task if ye render it in loving attitude of mind. Thus thine happiness or gloom emergeth from *THAT* state of mind.

"And as ye serve Him in the thrill of harmony and content, when He steps aside to let thine experience in Cosmos garner greater Truth, let not go of His Hand until He frees thine and finds the soul strong, stable well learned in His Way and fit to walk alone. For if ye wander off to follow another without stronghold, in thy dull pain of remorse ye shall retrace thy steps, feeling the lack of Him Who is the Light and the Way; and search for Him anew, for ye left a part of thine own self behind, that anchor of spirit, that ye shall remember when all else is forgotten. Walk humbly with thy God.

"We assure Guidance to one and all, We counsel him who

would listen. Our Teaching is a tool, a road-mark, that he who follows may find liberation. We thank thee."

In the Order of Melchisedec
We are
—YOUR ELDER BROTHERS—

Chapter Five

At the Hem of Holy Garments

"And every spirit that confesseth not that Jesus Christ is come in the flesh is not of God; and that spirit of antichrist, wherefore ye have heard that it should come, and now already is in the world." (I John 4:3)

The Living Master Jesus

It is said "a living master comes into every age" but the Love of Jesus, His Light, still shine into the heart of mankind after two thousand years. He is and remains Lord of Earth and of Man until another of equal Esteem takes on the Mantle and Post.

The Word Christ means Light. It is the all-pervading Christ Consciousness, though called by other names. It is easy for the lifelong worshipper to get bored and look for more exciting outlets; of God as they may be they also lead to other depth in the end.

Jesus the Lord and the Light-Consciousness are as real to me as flesh and blood, thinking and breathing, for I sat at His Feet, journeyed far beyond lower worlds and many universes, to find the Reality of Him and God within the soul. He spoke to me as He will to anyone who cares enough to lay aside the little self and would manifest required conditions. Though the Body of Christ appears in many robes there is no mistake as to Who He is and no one appears to you in His stead, though masters ascended and unascended walk among us. The Face of the Shroud of Turin appeared to me in Living, Celestial Flesh. I cannot forget. Though I've met the Master many times on journeys to worlds beyond and encountered the living manifestation of Holy Beings, the Face of Jesus the Christ was the most soulful experience. Total Peace, Strength, Glory, Perfection, Wisdom, Love, Mercy, and Protection, all these combined shone from His Radiant Features, none can compare. It invoked a feeling of *total* trust, there was nothing left to fear, in this life or the next. This happening sets forever free.

The feeling it leaves with you has no interpretation. Longing, restless seeking, doubt, inner churning, yearning, weeping, and zeal are suddenly swept away as all paths that lead to God have run into the *ONE*. The psychic search is over, what predictive stars proclaim no longer holds true, the meaning of salvation remains but a Word. Wherever that unspeakable Love of Christ would lead you, even if it were to the pits of hell and disaster, you would follow without fear or question for you know nothing can touch you, nothing at all. And should the Presence ask of you to follow Him Homeward in that moment or thereafter it wouldn't be a day too soon. His total Peace reigns Omnipresent, Omnipotent!

Months before, He suddenly stood suspended and tall as a tower in the midst of inner skies—The Son of God—His Hands raised in blessing. The Face was turned a bit to the right, His Hair was dark and closely cropped to the head, the out-billowing gigantic folds of His Mantle shone in the brightness of a thousand suns. He vanished from view as quickly as He came. For weeks on end I questioned: "Who are You?" until I remembered the scripture: "Prove thou me!" and began to demand the truth as though all else depended on it. I didn't really expect an answer. In an unexpected moment His Face appeared in unthought of revelation. Still I didn't know Who it was that induced my transformation and left me so utterly assured of Holy Succor. That same evening while busy with my files I layed some papers on my desk and strangely kept one in my hand while rearranging the rest. Suddenly a trembling ran through me, tears ran down my face for no reason, for I held in my hand a crumbled up picture that I had saved for ten years, of the Face of the Christ of Turin. And then I knew. The Face was identical to the Face that graced my solitude, especially the nose, forehead, the mouth. What can I say? It changed my life. Over the years I examined many paths, the left path, right path and under-path if you will. Being so blinded by the wool pulled over my eyes of a "quick" path to God I even thought the story and life of Jesus was but a comforting anecdote and though I experienced His Living Presence many times, the answer still remained a question. Once the Voice asked: "Why do you doubt Me?" But now I knew! Of course the noble scholar might say what I saw was illusion but Truth becomes your Reality, regardless.

This does not take away from the experience that remains ever so personal and profound. It does not mean that the deep devotion or belief of another person is error, for the heart of him may be purer than that of all the rest even if he never heard of Christ; even as the bushman feels embued by Magnificent Spirit, feels the utter Glory of Redemption and calls it ah, so good! In the end this is what opens Inner Gates and lets the spirit enter. But you may be very sure that the pure in heart walk in and out of heaven worlds at will, while still in physical embodiment, whether by Grace, or spontaneous out-of-body projection or soul-travel with the Master or perhaps they leave the body by innate instinct and at will; as did every true saint. The Seventh Sacrament, Soul-Travel, is a very part of the true spiritual life.

Unlike Gurus that suddenly pop up from modern day mystery schools and claim to be saviors, a Living Master as Jesus is a being of holiness, worthiness, who has taken up a physical body to bring total liberation to unascended lifewaves in the lower physical universe. A true Living Master is free of vice, attachments and has overcome every desire of the physical flesh, being wedded to the Divine in every sense of the word, for this is His holy allegiance. He is self-sustaining and never supported by donations from His followers or peers. Gentle and kind, He is endowed with every Divine Virtue, never looks down or belittles other servers, for He knows the Light within Him shall teach the heart. You know a Living Master is real when you are in soul-body and meet Him in the God-Worlds, see Him standing garmented in Celestial Light that at times is so bright it hurts the spiritual eyes. You shall see such a One teaching the multitudes and there will be no doubt as to Who He is. This is the True Master. Yet it is not the Radiant Form that is the Master but the Holy Spirit of God occupying the Holy Being, *THAT IS* the Master, that sheds Its own radiance through the spiritual flesh.

All others you meet on earth are teachers unascended, even though they may be pristine vessels. Masters walk among us, those who have conquered the world of the personal self. Perhaps they wear a human cloak, they are the angels you meet 'unaware.' There are those who would capably lead a spiritual humanity to better destinations, but regardless of their promise none shall carry you at the final hour across the River Styx, the dark river of Death—but Christ the Light, the Lord. Each must earn this Grace for himself if he would bypass the Lords of Death.

Jesus was the God-Man Who became the Christ, Master of Perfection through His own regeneration, the divine estate every soul shall attain, to this end we were born. He as any other soul endured cycles of reimbodiments, attained Masterhood Consciousness and through His Christship, Lordship in spiritual government. He taught the doctrine of reincarnation to His true followers, as even our Christian forefathers taught reincarnation. And when He said: "Before Abraham was I AM, but ye knew Me not," He devoutly referred to the Great I AM Presence within Him, the Eternal "I"—the IT, the Formless Creator, that was before the Beginning and is the Essence of *all* life, now, tomorrow and for all Eternities to come.

Jesus the Christ never asked to be deified nor did He wear the ecclesiastic robes of the literary, of the heathen, neither did He call Himself savior, although He was the very last of a long lineage of saviors before Him who as He sought to save man from himself. The Teachings of Jesus pointed to the divinity and immortality of the soul, which opposes the theory of "the wretched worm of the dust" since the latter would find little purpose in living and no realms of glory awaiting it after physical death.

The Consciousness of Christ is the Divine Spirit, Its Essence flows through every creation in any universe or world. This selfsame Spirit is waiting to be reawakened and reborn in the manger of every heart and only in the full realization of this Impersonal "I" does "My yoke become easy and My burden light." The yoke is not lifted by Jesus the Lord, it must be layed to rest by the individual self. It is said: "there is no cross" but there is, for He, bearing His own, demonstrated that every soul must shoulder its own responsiblities, yet, by the weight of His Cosmic Mission He lifted the darkness of all. When He translated He not merely died for the redemption of the 'lost' but for Himself as well; which was part of the Divine Plan and not a blunder.

Therefore no one can die to save another and no one ever will, save we die to our horrid hatreds, greeds, passions of the flesh, meanness of spirit and other self/overindulgences. Those who lament from pulpits that Jesus the Christ died to save the world need but look around to see a humanity in great distress, for nothing, nothing, nothing is saved, in fact the present lifewave is worse than the one before. Conditions all around cry out for redemption as sickness of body, mind and soul plague the world-soul persistently and avarice, infernal wars and self-destruction pervade the scene.

The Consciousness of Christ is the consciouness of the twice-born, the awakened *I AM*, God-Presence within the regenerated being. This is the Wine, Bread of Life, Living Waters and "open door that no man can shut" the Door to Heaven, within the consciousness of man. There is no other door, there never was. To set diverse teachings to order, may it be realized that truth belongs where it is. Even as we "cannot add one cubit to our stature" to deduct from Divine Reality is equal folly.

Jesus the Christ embodied a far Greater Power and frequency of Divine light than anyone after Him could endure, lest the physical form would disintegrate. Saints and saviors before Him transfigured and ascended as He, but none to date since Him gained this lofty plateau of being, their discarded bodies rest in graves. We honor all noble souls that followed the Master's Footsteps, who left us a legacy of examplary living. We merely counsel the true seeker to know Who and what a True Living Master is, that he my look to that Divine Source of all Power and Master of masters: God's Holy Spirit.

When one meets this Great Lord embodied by Majesty, the soul no longer walks by faith but by sight and it is never an emotional experience but a distinct reality that rends the fog from wayward beliefs. The Master-Light appears in your forehead, even a spark of It unfolds the soul in the Radiant Love of Christ.

Only adventurous, daring souls will leave the physical body at will to learn to die in order to know how to live, thusly they worship 'in spirit and in truth.' Many hear the Master's Word, the Sound, in the quiet recesses of their heart and life never remains the same while others wait "until bleached bones lie scattered on the sands of time" and another reimbodiment affords a new opportunity to learn a better way.

—THE AUTHOR—

Take No Thought

"Children of Light;

"Take no thought of what the day shall bring, neither be weary, for I tread softly, come into your aid and stand at the Open Door. As *I AM* in the Father, you are also in Him in the Oneness of His Essence. All you are cometh into My Light and if my answer remaineth a question, I trust you walk in courage and in faith.

"Why do you doubt Me while at the same time you ask My Intervention? If doubt assails, look to the Light of your being, you shall find Me there. When you reach for My Hand, it has already touched yours, I never withdrew it. When in your heart-pain you turn to Me, the Rays of My Heart fall into yours to soothe the torrent. When your earthly bread is meager and your lamentations fierce, it is because you have not reached for the Bread I offered you that would still your cravings and hunger and because you have not yet realized that when you ask it in My Name it has already been provided. My Good flows through every human experience.

"Your dire want is My opportunity to make you aware of My Presence, *I AM* always with you, I never left. The table is set, if you would but come!

"You know Me as a warmth that ripples through your being, the Love beyond words that mists your eyes, I AM the Light that shines through your loving, giving and through every charitable action; for I within you *AM* expressing as you!

"When your vision has cleared away doubt and disbelief you shall see Me as *I AM* and talk to Me face to face, for this is My Covenant with you, not in your imagination but in My Reality, then you may command Me to appear and it shall come to pass. Though you withdraw from Me for a time, I shall come again and again into every new awakening until I receive you unto Myself. You may follow other masters but you will critically compare them with My perfection and come back into My Arms. I gave to each a choice and a Way by which to become free. Only in the freedom of My Light can you find yourself in Me, for *I AM THAT*—which you are.

"You are the creator of your immediate conditions and of your tomorrows in the eternal *NOW*, often it is that from which you seek escape. Your freedom seeking nature must grant freedom to others if you are to retain yours. Neither oblige nor join when wrong is committed against you, keep yourself harmless in forgiveness, then constant peace shall be your noble companion. You cannot lash out and swart without feeling its retribution. Take heed not to neglect the simple things I ask of you, for of what value are proud accomplishments when you are taken back to the bottom rung of the ladder to start anew? To learn a lesson over!"

The Still Small Voice

"You have been given the counsel of My still small voice, its words are clear when the feeling self unfolds in Grace. It is the nudging of instant approval and reproval within your own conscience that you quickly perceive. Therefore treat not with others of what shall be, for the Teacher speaks clearly, distinctly through your inner being. And do not even ask Me, for *I AM* within His Voice the audible answer. *I AM* the shining Light that teaches you to love by Loving Me, that in loving yourself you would endure and rectify to make straight the crooked path.

"No matter how grave the error of commission or omission, no matter how self-degrading the deed, in self-forgiveness you are forgiven, for it is the all-forgiving God-Aspect within you. The Holy Comforter speaks to you through My Voice and Mine through yours, that the heart may sing the lovesong of a sparkling, clean conscience; and hope and cheerfulness would grant a fuller, richer life. The Voice sings a Melody when you perk up the inner ear and hearken to Its small whisperings. Then you may come to Me as often as you wish carried by Its Power. I safeguard from the tempest, in Me is rest and peace and I say, it is better to be innocent than penitent, purity is loveliness unto God when the wayward self has come into My Light. Through carnal frustrations and confusion the negative self seeks control, it drains away energy, clouds the realistic goal as brewing anger rests and lingers underneath every good intention, undermines your efforts. I inspire you to love, that now you may look calmly, confident upon the turbulence of testing conditions. Self-discipline inspires right thinking, you think and create! The shuttle of the mind throws thoughts hither and yon' like birds thrown out of the nest that scream and scatter in all directions. The thought-threads you weave into the web of life bind or set free, for, the Cosmic

Spindle picks up the thread, adds to it yet another of like virtue of good or ill and what you weave becomes the cloak you alone must endure. I say, listen to My still small Voice, drop wornout threads to take on better ones that Love and Faith may be the weaver of a shining cloak. And verily, I say, what seemeth right to the senses by heavenly Precepts may chance error while what you deem useless may prove a Great Blessing in the Unseen. Endeavor not to run toward better cirumstances and from present responsibilities rather attain to the need of the hour to be spared self-undoing; for when you are in the present is the place I have prepared for you.

"My Beloved, let your tenth be laid into the palms of the poor, not into baskets where thieves divide the spoil, for verily, then shall life manifest goodness in your knowingness that *I AM* the Giver and the Hand giving through yours. Thus you shall grow content! In your contentment is found no unrest or malice, for it holds in itself no thought of wrong, right, evil, or good and being content if a thought disturbeth thee, turn from it quickly, it is in your power! When you draw into My Harmony and willingly accept what in necessity must be given you shall no longer suffer vexation of spirit but grow in a blessedness that weaves a faultless pattern into your seamless Robe.

"My Beloved Children, rise to the Perfection of the Father, for He even spoke to Job: Be thou perfect! The Eternal SELF was before the Beginning, your shining Self—from which Deity shines forth as a blazing beacon-light that pierces all darkness. When you gaze at this light within your forehead and come into My harmony, I will inspire you to serve Me, you are *THAT* need, that cause, that Blessing! Therefore *I AM* also the effect to each cause that rebounds to your actions. Only in My Cause shall you return to the First Cause and become whole, the Way and the Light, in which you shall learn to love Me as yourself. *I AM* expressing as you, look not for Me, I never left!

"Those who serve My Purpose in self-adulation, endearment of idolatries and fruitless joy soon call out for a Miracle that I may bring the restless wanderer into My Peace. Beloved hearts, there are no miracles or miracle workers, My Holy Spirit, My Breath of Life is the *ONLY* Miracle Worker that pours through Its vessels in the moment of need: that sutleers and swaggers misuse until in seeming abandonment of spirit and desolation they lament: 'If He died for my sins, why am I paying for them?' Which brings them closer to My Truth. Thus, Spirit ploughs and seeds the barren field of carnality, subdues the egocentricity of man, that he who heretofore sought the consolation of the damned would turn to Me to find the way out from within—which calls for necessary detachment from the prideful emotional arena.

"In your devotion some of you have the idea to please Me requires you to be continually altruistic, but this is a psychological perception and serves no one, to do nothing would serve Me better, for each must find its own true Self within Me, where I take the outstretched hand and guide it beyond its own shadow into the Light.

"You have inhabited body after body, life after life. Some of you exited life through the back door in a guilt that plagued into deathless death for you denied My Counsel. Again some of you stand at the same crossroad contemplating another way out, lo, I say, ye may find it in *ME*! The inaction of deep sadness calls for counteraction of active contemplation in the Light, for in *that*, ye overcome the tempest, find a life worth living. You have plumbed the heights and depth of endless groping for My Reality and now found Me in your True Noble Self. And I shall pour My Quickening upon you and everyone that being quickened you shall pour it forth to the deprived and poor in heart, for I dwell in all. You shall meet with scoffing, with persecution of the vile, but remain in My Peace that transcendeth understanding. For you shall see Me in their eyes, hear My answer through their voice and know only Me.

"For as all elements embody My Essence and the firmaments proclaim My Glory and all substance finite and Infinite declare My Truth, all is born, reborn and redeemed in this selfsame Consciousness of Light.

"In the still, clear Respites that lay as quiet ponds in the Nameless void of Cosmos, you shall experience reflections of My Countenance and Reality as *YOURSELF*, hear the Melody of your True Nature shall crown your life with contentment and the blessing of every constructive purpose and righteousness shall permeate your being like an overflowing stream. You need neither mediator nor intercessor, only the willingness to live in the constancy of Light that is the Presence within you.

I AM the Dweller at the Threshold, the Way, Truth and Life of your being, that was and *IS*, your own God-Self. From the deep, vast center of My Countenance shineth a Light, the Light is YOU in divine aspect, Lo, *I AM* with you always.

"*I AM* come into your cause, I bear you forever in My Light. *BE STILL* and *KNOW—I AM THAT!*"

I AM —JESUS—

Messengers of the Absolute

Truth tends to dishearten and disillusion us, too often we fail to perceive its subtle blessing, such is the nature of the personality. But Truth threads its fine, invisible essence through all manner of consciousness that we may adhere to its teachings, attuned to Higher Dimensions. The unfamiliar, even though it may be our hidden security, leaves us insecure until we fill our void with another comfort. We're not too eager to change ingrained, traditional beliefs that forbid communication with the Messengers of God. But how did Holy Scriptures come into being, if not channeled through man? God is "no respector of persons!"

As not to crack the mold of our indoctrinations we shelve the subject until the gales of life chill us to the bone and then we welcome anything and *any* Voice that might bring us into a more favorable climate. Worse, we accept unreliable inner voices at the spur of a frantic moment—which lead into the dregs of spiritism and unfortunately more grief. Just because some of the living population of Beyond tries to help, they have no better advice than those of earth, in that they do not all dwell in Lands of Higher Consciousness. The ungenerated mind picks up voices and texts from electronic ethers that are mostly thoughts of other minds, or from lower astral planes. As much as the listening Angel adheres itself to the prayerful devotee, likewise entities of darkness enter dialogues with the spiritually deprived.

It is of uttermost importance that we deepen our perception of God's Shining Host to know our source of information. Religious teachers and occultists alike claim that God never speaks through anyone, while they themselves publish their dialogues with the Divine and claim to have the answer for the salvation of mankind. God never speaks directly to anyone, for the Absolute creator is not the God of Abraham and Jacob but the Formless Being and Principal source of all Life, and speaks to us through the Counsel of Angels, Ascended Masters, Avatars, and Lords that serve Spiritual Government and rule myraids of sunlit worlds and hundreds of existing Universes.

Each individual world is ruled by a Glorious Lord, each universe by a Logoi and all Intelligences are Messengers of the Absolute Creator through Whom He, *THE IT*—communes *within* us through Intelligences via the Audible Lifestream. Its Audible Current can be heard by everyone. It is the True Word of God. Stepped down in voltage and greatly modified, the silent listener can gather up direct knowledge and compile it into a text. Thusly all Holy Scriptures came into being until they were altered to suit carnal purposes.

The Audible Life Current can be heard in the undertone of every conversation and is felt as an outflowing vibration from every living thing. You hear it in the wind, the downpouring rain, in the ocean roar, the chirping birds, the buzzing of bees, to name just a few, as a deep Humming *HU*. When still a small child, I would run out into the woods and stand among the tall pines to hear the snow fall. Suddenly I heard a Melody within the sound of the falling snow, what it was I didn't know, it infilled me with unspeakable joy and made me see another World in a life everlasting. When I asked others if they heard it, they found me very peculiar, though I never gave details.

The Sound is a wondrous Melody in Its Higher Octaves, a soul-stirring Music, this Sound of God. It is the wordless language no one can convey, save the one who hears and knows and what he knows is for himself alone no matter how ardently he wishes to share it. It remains a personal experience, the unwritten Dialogue embossed upon the tablets of the sacred heart. It thrills the hearer to the finest atom, human and divine, and leaves behind the ecstasy that Saints called *LOVE*.

Without this melodic Current no life can exist, it is Life Itself. All we are and ever can be is sure forth out of this Lifestream. All the Love we are capable of expressing, all constructive and destructive powers of Nature are Its Energy, for God is energy and energy is God. In the physical-material universe in modified manifestation It redeems Itself by what it leaves behind or *undone*. The Divine Current of the Audible Lifestream is called by religions the Holy Spirit, without further explanation of what It is. Those who hear the Melody and feel the cold heat of Its Current become spirit-filled for that moment. Instant healings occur by Its Touch, whether it flows through a serving channel or directly through the petitioner or through consciousness en masse. One can hardly speak of or write about It and not experience Its permeating Power. This living, golden energy of the Audible Lifestream threads Itself through everything It created, for It IS Its own creation in every sense, Essence of Creation and Co-Creation.

The pearl of consciousness is the innate part of Its Body through which Love, Wisdom and Truth flow. It diffuses and infuses every branch and artery of universes and worlds without end and every spiritual teaching and system. So we can hardly say which path is right or wrong in that all aspire to the same goal and every Godward Way serves Its ultimate Purpose, except that we may find the clear meaning of Beingness directly through the Inner Way, that short-circuits the listless search and frees from the endless Wheel of Involution, reincarnation, life after life.

Jesus the Christ referred to this Lifestream as: "This is the true light which lighteth every man coming into the world...marvel not that I said unto thee, ye must be born again...that which is born of flesh is flesh, that which is born of spirit is spirit.... Verily, verily, I say unto thee, except a man be born again, he cannot see the Kingdom of God." (John 1:9, St. John 3:7, St. John 3:8, John 3:) And he spoke of the Sound, saying: "The wind bloweth where it listeth and thou hearest the Sound thereof; but canst not tell whence it cometh and whither it goes; so is everyone that is born of the Spirit." (St. John 3:8)

"I am the light of the world. He that followeth me shall not walk in darkness, but shall have the light of life."(John 8:12)

"Now ye are clean through the Word [the Sound] which I have spoken unto you."(John 15:3)

The Word comes to us through the Sound Current of the Audible Lifestream, Jesus referred to Light and Sound being one, that is the all-purifying Bread and Water of Life.

The I-ness of the Absolute pours forth Its Message from the Center of Its Being—the Ocean of Love and Mercy. It may shock us out of complacency to realize that the Formless Creator does not interfere with human conditions. It does not even care. But it gave us the tool of consciousness, Light and Sound by which we have liberation. Once you hear the Clarion Call of the Audible Lifestream, life never remains the same. Its loveliness and constructive revelations speak from deep chambers of the heart through Intelligences of High Esteem; not through whispering, fading voices but in clear sentences and impressions that flow in on the Sounds of Soul. We feel the Presence, the Law and Lord of Our Being and the Love which is the underlying true Essence of all beliefs and *CHRIST*—ian teachings. It is *A LOVE*—self-emptied of any other.

Sunlit worlds of inspiration open their portals. When in the deep silence of prayer the soul forgets the physical world; and vision and being flow out within sound and light into the Arms of the everlasting Presence. The Sound becomes the Word of God that moves upon the waters of the sacred soul, to bring it into His Radiant Purpose. And we shall hear what a Lord has to say in the following dictation that I recorded with the pen of my heart.

The Sound of God Moves Upon the Waters

"Love thou Me with all thine heart, serve thou Me in the power I shall grant thee. By whatever Name ye call Me, I AM the Comforter, the Holy Breath of My own Being, Redeemer to every soul, there is none beside Me.

"Seek Me not in mortal teachings, thou shalt not find Me in imperfections, but look to the soul that ye may find Me there well established as ye remove thy effort, thy thought, thy will, and thyself! There is none beside Me and without Me ye can do nothing. I AM He that dwells in the spaceless Void. In the smallest ensoulment I AM the Prism Light that I remold or dispose of as I choose.

"I AM the Message through the messenger who claims to be Myself. Believe not in messianic figures, those aflame with pride who wish to stand out from the rest, I have only chosen their vessel to give forth glimpses of My Reality. Be prepared to know, not all who teach are of the Light. Most are dangerously inadequate, basking in egocentricity they call themselves masters in My Name. Ye shall see them egested, as shall be with all that steal My Glory! Everyone that holds stewardship is a hireling, subject to fall for he has not been made perfect in Me. Sit not at tables of idolatry in worship!

"In thy distress call upon thy Guardian Spirit I sent to care for thee. Treat not with him who denies the Christ who would take His place on earth as a leader, for if I withdraw from such a one ye shall see he barely liveth by his unsanctified life-threads. My Voice speaketh to thee through earth teachers to serve *MY* Cause, not to serve his greed. Look only to *THAT,* that floweth through him for the moment, that is not man, woman nor the container, but *MY PRESENCE*—'Thou shalt have no other gods before Me!'

"Ye know the Way by which the saints shall bring thee unto Me, and if ye claim My Saints have no power, why doest thou pray to them by beaded strings for intercession? If ye believe heaven is a state of mind, why do ye pray to enter it? Ye fear rising from thy center, for thy heart perceiveth Me not. Ye fear death but what ye deem as death and loss is but a change in course of the eternal voyage of thine immortal self. Fear not death, for as ye are absent from the body ye are present within ME. I AM the Lord of thy body, how can it be otherwise? My Law is unchangeable. Attend ye to the soul, for all thy hands hold shall quickly perish and leave thee only the strand of a memory in other realities.

"Consider the vastness of time passed and the length of it before thee, in thy useless, debilitating fears to lose the unreal if thou doest not feel the unreal how can pain or grief befall thee when the soul liveth? How can ye feel harm when ye never perished? What disturbeth thee? Are ye not willing to leave the unreal for a small space to enter the fullness of My Life? Verily, I affirm My Law demonstrated by My Beloved Son Jesus through the Only Begotten Spirit that liveth within thee forevermore, proved the soul does rise and IS even now, by which ye may come apart. And if ye refuse to rise awake and aware from thy house of clay ye prove thine unbelief in Me. For in coming apart ye would forsaken they little selves to behold the distortions of thy life as well as My Grace.

"My Voice speaketh from thy holy tabernacle, from whence I enmantle thee with Love, there ye may eat My Bread and place My Wine to thy lips. I oversee thy comings and thy goings, whom shall ye fear? My Message is written upon every fiber of thy being, so is My Name, My Love abideth forever! Believe not in messengers, for I AM the Messenger that speaketh through them to thee, there is none beside *ME*!

"The priestcrafts admonish how ye ought to live while they

do otherwise. They take thy bread but break it not with thee and if thy fellows praise thee they shall turn and quickly condemn thee. And if mayhaps they drop thee a coin and ye refuse it, lo, ye shall feast with the Gods. And I counsel thee, My Children, while intellects stand robed in long garments uttering Love and Law, they use their power of madness to control thee, outwardly and within thy resting spirit, of that ye know not. Their devastation shall be great. Give thyself in reflection, ponder My Sayings, that ye might grow wise and simple and life would be more fit for thee. And in thy ponderance, Who can deliver but ME?

"Ye have power to live free of compulsion and complexity if ye decree: 'Let there be Light!' If ye demand it, it shall be given for the Light is the Christ ye call upon, the call giveth the answer, prove thou *ME*!—And thy labors shall beget purpose and thy mind be freed of the Shadow.

"Within thy being ye hold the secret doctrine of My immutable, unchanging Law. Within thy finer being ye may tap the springs of Creation to grow strong and there give ear to the Sound, the Word, of the Host of My Estate that I send to teach thee. And though each step forward be harder than the last, if ye keep My Statute, the elements of My First Principle and Cause shall do thy bidding. As ye walk in My Way all-accepting, I shall grant thy perfection destination in Me that ye may be rich. When ye have left thy wasteful emotions of hate, left thy proud enterprising behind and bring thy self-emptied cup, it shall be heaped up to pouring over and ye shall not despair.

"When ye link the soul to Mine in the radiance of wordless prayer, ye become My Thoughts, My Voice and I shall christen thee to speak with the tongue of Angels and carry My Light into the world upon that My Holy Spirit has come upon thee. Ye are precious in My Sight, every one, I love thee no matter how irritated, gross and obstinate ye may be. Deep in thy heart liveth My Grace, My own Ideal of Selflessness of service and Lover and in mutual consent to serve, My Cause shall come to fruition, that ye would care less for the small self and more for the rest.

"My Children of High Esteem, guard the pearls of Wisdom ye receive from My Council, for the tyrant shall seek to destroy, and if ye would destroy evil, ye must do so being stationed in Light and forsake every sense of personal power. Then shall neither good nor evil affect, as ye keep thyself harmless of both. For oft' good leadeth to greed and grief which is darkness also. Then My Light shall neutralize malignant forces from within and without, mark ye well, It spareth not the atom!

"When ye come to Me in thy finer flesh ye shall understand the great magnitude of molecular energy, the fine electrical waves of the Light; that ye may gather unto thyself or dispose of to do thy bidding. The Life, the Essence is thine own Self. For while in the aberration and rhythm of dense matter ye claim it to be anti-light or light anti-matter, ye know not truth; for, what truth is to one, may not be fact in the Unseen. When ye no longer wager between good and evil, ye shall know the proper use of the velocity of Light, the Current by which ye may consciously, fully aware—come unto Me. *I AM* within each and everyone the Fountain of all Good, the Grace, Mercy and Life, if thou wouldst come to receive."

I AM—THE LORD—
OF THY BEING

Flames of Pentecost

The subject of speaking in tongues has been a mystery to many. Over the years I marveled at the hysteria of conversion and over-emotionalism by which some rolled on the floor kicking up their heels, shouting and tearing at their hair. I prayed never to be subject to such tastless behavior so as not to make a spectacle of myself, after all, I was raised right and simply wouldn't allow it. More than once I said such carrying on was a disgrace to God. When it happened to me I had to live with my own words and forget my false pride, and saw the subject of speaking in tongues in a different light. I still contend that the Holy Spirit is always in control, It does not advocate disgusting behavior, BUT, this may depend on time and place and to some degree of self-control—if possible.

It is truly a rapturous experience and I guess one doesn't really know what sets it off, save devotion and genuine surrender. It can overcome a person quite unexpectedly, as do the bursts of illuminations and initiations that follow that accompany our inner growth. Since the Divine is my central focus it is natural that very little can rouse me out of the quietudes of inner ventures, supplications or prayer, though at times the outer world can ruffle my peace-filled way of being. There is much to give account of and time too short and precious to be squandered on other endeavors. Often the little self reared its pride-filled head when I asked the Divine Spirit would never overcome me in public as it was experienced in the privacy of my home. I still feared the spectacle!

When it occurs I feel a definite Presence, a Power that envelopes me with great pressure, at times pushes me down to my knees. One time it knocked me from the kitchen into the front room and I landed face down, too scared to move. The noble scholar might call it an astral force, but this is not so, for the Force I know is *LOVE* and a feeling of a cleansed heart only God can give, if but for the moment. Then, it felt as though It had a hold of my tongue, it spoke in an unknown language in the wisdom of Angels that I understood but couldn't put into words. In fact it magnified Itself as though a hundred tiny, flaming tongues were speaking all at once, but from an Inner, Higher Dimension and I was there, it was sunlit and bright. When the Voice became still, I entered profound calmness; in that total composure I can barely move and the interpretation begins. So, "not being present in body but present in the Lord," who knows what the rest does?

Once I thought perhaps to retain the awareness of mind to turn on the tape-recorder in an effort to recapture what was being said, but it does not work this way, there is no time to press a button while the Force enters the being.

My first experience of speaking in tongues occurred when a thankful person brought me a religious medal that she found in an old empty house. I layed it on the shelf for a few days. Finally, touching the medal of Jesus I could feel it permeated by a strange light, it made me light-headed, also, the sense of touch revealed to inner senses that the object may have hung around the neck of a dead body. So I sat quietly for a moment to demagnetize the vibrations. No sooner than my prayer began, a force lifted me into the warm Light of Spirit, where I beheld the full materialization of Jesus. The Power spoke in a foreign language, I trembled to the smallest atom as it shook me like a flimsy rag. Again I felt a pressure on my throat and the Voice gave the interpretation of what had been given that a visiting friend heard as well. It stopped as suddenly as It came. It surprised me to feel my face wet with tears, especially since I had no recollection of physical or emotional sensations. My friend wept too.

After this happening the ecstasy of tongues reoccurred frequently and even a simple prayer would be taken over by the Force that finished it, speaking in tongues. It is never a self-induced state, it is felt by the brush of an unseen wind and a rolling heat going through the physical form. This is how it starts, at least it is so with me. This moved me to read about this phenomenon, but nothing at all described what I felt inside. So I asked the Divine Spirit for a direct answer, perhaps some specifics on the subject, the following was given:

Speaking in Golden Tongues

"Write, O Beloved, songs of deliverance, take an uncompromising stand against self-pride. Open wide the Gate of soul to give entrance to the Holy Ghost, that the dross may be caught up into Its floatage and carried off by Its fanning into the Vacuum of purification. You can hear the skirts of the Mother-Light sweep across the garden of the heart, it gathers up the roses of your devotions. In Love you shall enter the cool heat of Flames of Pentecost in the unsealment of Golden Tongues that were given to the Twelve in like manner.

"Come, come, Beloved to that High Place of Wonder where the Angel stands with the flaming torch at the Gate of the Heavenly Eden. Bring your candle to the Altar of Time and He shall ignite the flickering spark to soaring flame, infuse your vestures of light with the rose-glow of Love that weaves the bridal garment and your coarser fibers shall be made whiter than driven snow. When your body is at rest, Beloved, you meet the Christ in your finer flesh, wander free into the God-Life where He cleanses and quickens the life-force, and life upon earth shall be more fit for thee. And even if hope seems dashed to pieces and the material world crumbles about, hold fast to the Christ and Law of your being, it shall regrant! Wisdom is Love, is Power, is Trinity, Three in One, inseparable One. Within this Trinity you find the burden released, more importantly the renunciation of self. There, the Spirit of God moves upon the waters of soul, of spirit and opens the floodgates to the baptismal insurging of the Holy Ghost.

"It does not promise pockets of gold but a gladness that abideth forever. I say, be not entrenched nor content with what you learn here or there of truth, not all assertions are a spiritual fact nor Reality. Thus in desparity, gloom and discouragement you cannot blame another, for the teacher was taught yet by another who knew less than the first. The Truth you seek is found in the silence of Spirit where the White Light of Grace satisfies all longing. He, the Holy Comforter, is Teacher, you need none other. Verily, in Him you garner the newness of spirit that permeates your life with perpetual joy. The Light you see in your forehead is the Flame of God affirming your true estate. It bestows prophetic utterance after you have cleansed the carnal tongue of wasteful talk and all desire and all prejudgment have dissolved in the Light. Then you shall receive the Holy Ghost, the empowerment of Spirit, and your speech shall carry a royal ring as you speak in Golden Tongues and interpret what is given. And I, the Guardian of the Flaming Chalice, shall safeguard everyone, each that bringeth the beast to the manger of the heart to lay animal passion to rest, as even they of yore lay down before the King.

"The Lord of your being poureth His Spirit upon all flesh in the Sacrament of Tongues, yeah, even the babe speaketh with the tongue of the Angel, though you perceive it not! Withhold your sayings from the vulgar, the scoffer, who would trample divinity into dust. What is given, write upon parchments that others may grow wise. And if such is your gift in the Fires of Wisdom, say not: 'It cannot be done by me,' for you embody Him in Essence, Who alone giveth the increase after the haughtiness of intellect is layed aside. You are handmaidens and servants not by choice but by Grace.

"When in your giftedness you are unable to please, know it is your gift to Him and to none other. Fear not the vipers, serpents of human vicissitude, rather grow in knowing Him Who tests the spirit in man, aye, I say, tries and tampers it in the blaze of Pentecostal Fire. He knoweth the barrenness that besets the soul, the desolations that drew it unto Him, for ye come to Him driven or drawn. The assaults you suffer by virtue of the Shadow are your battle of Armageddon as it now is, and was from the Beginning, in that, you are not alone but aided by the Legions of Light.

"And though you speak with the voices of men, in that you are sanctified you now speak a language Divine. Then stand not unbelieving in wonderment if your mental world has fallen apart, but remain silent, for the soul has come into alignment with Him. Before, you said you were well being out of alignment and now in proper adjustment you feel, My Scribe, all is not well with thee? It is because the crooked fence is made straight and the prideful mind is in rebelllion!

"To answer your question: 'Why the necessity of speaking in tongues?' Beloved, you are not a stranger, nor foundling, but His own, born of the electronic God-Soul. Is it not reasonable He should call you by name in the *I AM* when He wishes to converse with His offspring and speak to you in Parental Language? Born of His Glorious Body, the Radiant Light, His Word can only manifest as the Sound moves across the electronic ethers of the soul. And as you understand what has been said, by this you know you are of God and those who are also His know, and interpret what is given.

"Paul spoke to the people of Corinth and said of the Word: 'And even things without life giving Sound...except they give a distinction in the Sounds how shall it be known what is piped or harped?' And moreover He spoke: 'Let all things be done to edifying...and let one interpret, but if there be no interpreter let him keep silent in the church and let him speak to himself, and unto God. For he that speaketh in an unknown tongue speaketh not unto men but unto God; for no man understandeth him; howbeit in the spirit he speaketh mysteries, but I would rather that ye prophesied for greater is he that prophesieth than he that speaketh unto men to edification and exhortation and comfort.'

"Beloved, you speak in languages of many lands, now, in rediscovery of divinity what is the language of soul but its Mother-Tongue? He who knows God speaketh the language of every creature! The language of every universe. His Word can be but a thought that pours forth en masse without a syllable, thus any soul in any land can hear it all at once, this is the Unspoken Word of Him Who knoweth, seeth and perceiveth even the slightest whisper or whimpering of His creatures. Are ye not more than these? Albeit ye rule them in Love.

"In the Spirit of Inspiration your goodly pen shall mark down a Great Truth, overshadowed by the Watcher of Pentecost. After reparation you shall sip of the Holy Grail, of the Nectar of the Gods, that shall enliven you with perfect intellect no matter what your former learning. You shall know the Way, as the narrow becometh broad and shining to the soul, read clearly the roadmap to Cosmic Highlands and discover the Secrets of the Bleeding Heart that is your own.

"Open the Door that the Virgin Spirit may enter your house, it is the lovely Light that broke forth from the Flame of the Eternal, from the Queen of Heaven that guardeth the spark. Then gladness shall be your constant companion, your lanterns of Light carry hope into the world, for how can you bring peace to the restless unless you found it within yourself? Your work is Cosmic, when you speak a holy utterance every creature in the vast Beyond shall perk up its ears and listen, for you were sanctified, baptized in the Fires of the Holy Ghost. I beseech one and all, wipe away every vile contention, all manner of scorning speech, edit thoughts and sentences to stand approved to God, for now you speak by empowerment of Spirit, 'less the Voice would grow silent.

"Break and burst the shackle that binds, despair not, neither give up, but dare to do right in the precepts of regeneration and a new life. The calming influence of the Force restores presence of mind and perfect poise that you shall realize the unlimited creativity within you. When others speak you will listen with the soul, speak thoughtfully in the language of the Just in discerning manner, for unlawful utterings bear consequence. Baptized in the Holy Ghost you now see by the Light of Heaven. Should the eye behold evil, behold, within that evil core flameth a tender light in need of redemption, but not for you to reform in *any* way. 'All souls are God's!' Demean not any lest ye would be judged. To the sharp-tongued, give calm conversation it turneth away wrath. Each time you give Love you send forth the Angel that shall manifest to you in return. The greatest Love you can give is that of the Light that beams forth from your deepest center, it is Christ, this IS Love, it takes no thought save that of Him that gave it.

"The immortal soul that casts down the bounty and delights of its Noble Esteem, it loses foothold and can no longer bridge the chasm to the Eternal until karmic adjustments are made.

What is Caesars' belongs to him, what is of Spirit to Spirit, this cannot change, what ye sow ye reap.

"Arise, O children of Light, come ye apart to be well anchored in the Word, in the Spirit of the Beloved, draw near, lose thyselves in Sound, in Light, to receive the Tongues of Pentecost in the Fires of the Holy Ghost. I thank You."

In the White Fires of Light
I AM
—A GUARDIAN OF THE FLAMING CHALICE—

Chapter Six

Obedience, the Key to Transformation

Elect Beings that speak to us through the spirit of this book, vary in presentation and charismatic flair according to individual esteem and spiritual rank of each Instructor. But the Essence of every dialogue and discourse blends with the same Ideal as Cosmic Hierophants offer regeneration and spiritual freedom to the human race.

Listening to the Sound and holy undertone of their Voices we can hear the drumbeat of spiritual liberation that calls for transformation, freedom from oppression and freedom from physical and spiritual bondage through regeneration of the self; that the Peace we pray for would first manifest within the individual heart.

Instructions presented to my Readers throughout this book were received of long ago during days and hours of my earnest seeking. The wonder of it is, that when the Master speaks through the conduit He touches the consciousness of all. Then, by coincidence or by divine intent we pick up a leaflet or a book that gives problem solving answers, consolation and holy peace.

Again the Master-Light shone through the cathedral of the Shining Self and through its stillness the Venerable Master spoke up:

Be Ye Transformed!

"This I say to all who carry the flaming torch of Freedom! I AM come with a Chalice that bears the Light that is the Eucharist of redemption. Relinquish your hopes, dreams and aspiration into the Sacred Flame that thy noble intents shall come to quick fruition. Then the soul must wait in governed poise to receive its good. Ye must reset thy goals to positive directions, to give in, give out, give up...what manner is this? Does it profit thee?

"I say not! It grants another box of question marks! Go forth,

Beloved, forge onward! Carry the oil of Love, the wick in thy lanterns well trimmed, that the Light may burst forth as the glare of a sun, whereby refractions and reflections illumine the face of soul and none shall find fault nor guile in thee but behold the Christ instead.

"If in My Law ye feel chastened, it is to remind thee to live in discernment concerning all things. Ye shall not break thy promise to God nor man, for as ye promise man ye promise Him who is even thine Self. Shallowness, trickery of thought and motive must be rooted out of the prideful nature. Get thee to the mountain of transformation, obedient to self-reform, wash thy face at the mountain spring and in light-filled ethereal brooks that run along the delicate line of sacred hills in inner estates, to wash away the stain of guilt, arbitration and inharmony. Ye are called to the fishermen of many after ye learned to cast thy nets into the deep waters of Spirit, clear and clean, and learned to tap its currents of power for the good of creation. Ye are Gods clothed in the rags of materialism, I say, Awaken O Sleeper! Ye are giants in Spirit and by the Power of the Word, the Sound of Light, the fierce tempest shall step aside to let thee pass. As ye see the Angel ye must face *ASURE* is Law.

"Exchange not thy crown of glory for the gold of Mammon, say not, Beloved, the way is too hard, for lo, to depart from it shall be harder. And if mayhaps ye found a thing more precious, bemoan not the loss of that without permanence. When the door to error is shut, thine true fidelity and loyalty pledged to Him, then My Light shall go before thee and depict thy destiny. When solar-light floods the earth thank for Life, when it declines at eventide thank Him for the Light that is ever with thee and now behind stand Legions and Orders of a Mighty Host ye may call on to attend thy cause.

"Children of God, ye minister in various professions, where matters not but how well! Whether in common ways, lowly place or in comforts of a mansion, it is the place assigned to thee for a time. To disdain the lowly task is hindrance as ye forget humility. Blessed is he who labors in what is set before him, without qualm or question.

"Beloved, shut thine ear-gates to the enticer, to babbling aspersions of false teachers that bespatter thee with lies, albeit thy ruin shall be found in the wreckage of thy good intentions.

I say, voice not the law of various scripts, it is better to hear and obey, for: 'The Words of the Lord are pure Words; as silver tried in the furnace of earth.' When the immortal soul listens, ye have victory and need not fear defeat nor suffer vexation. Thus ye may gather up Bounties of Wisdom and thine earthen vessels shall overflow.

"Repetitious instructions are needful, that remembering ye would grow wise. Sit still, listen with the ears of soul, be patient, do not rush off in a huff after more palatable sayings of the black artist or professed leader of the Light who promise a shortcut and salvation, there are no shortcuts to God, lest ye would cleanse thyself promptly and overcome the small self. He who sits in darkness by candlelight, even he who claims prestige in the Light gives half-witted promise and by clever maneuvers and public display obscures from thee Eternal Truth. The black artist attempts to devalue the Holy Essence of Spirit by means of magical manipulations in all manner of psychic paranormal intrigue. Bewitchers boil worms and lizard tails to a develish brew by which they conjure up malignant forces to mend or destroy matter; while pseudo masters bombard the sleeper with *raw* adulterated energy and call themselves leaders of ancient esteem. Woe unto them, the Lord, the Law shall not hold them blameless and thus it stands written upon Eternal Ethers:

> "I charge thee before God, and the Lord Jesus Christ, and the elect Angels, that thou art observing these things. And some men's sins are opened before hand, going before judgment; and some men they follow after. Likewise also the good works of some are manifested before hand; and they that are otherwise cannot be hid." Scripture

"Bearers of Light, I counsel thee in the Spirit of God, forsake false doctrines, soothsayers and apocalyptic doom watchers who shout Grace down from Heaven and souls into the remnants of hell. They hold His sheepfold in fangs of ignorance and withhold My Counsel of Light, professing It. They never knew Me. Their ecclesiastic utterings and ancient babblings lead to craggy reefs of frustration that pierce him who taught falsely and him who listened to his vile contensions.

"Be ye renewed by the Fires of the Holy Ghost to receive the anointing of Spirit, for ye shall see the day when the earth shall be governed by Souls of Light, even before the Day of His Coming which to some shall be the coming of the Light as it is upon thee even now. Through the Fires of Divine Alchemy and transformation ye hear My Call: Obey the Mandate, forsake all vice, be ye transformed! And embued by His Magnificent Radiance it shall connect thee to the Pure Sound and the dissonance of dithyrambs shall be silenced. O Seeker, hold fast to the Light, it is resurrection, it is Life, the Way of the Life-Current by which ye enter the Worlds of God and become cognizant of thine true heritage. Thy greater destination is in view even now.

"Christ Intent is found everywhere, is seen in every need, in every good and honest joy, it appears in lowliness as in loveliness for It Is. When ye feel bereft of Our Attention, it is that ye should use the strength of the innate Light and learn to stand alone without wavering. In thy faithful contemplations and deep perception of the Light it shall burst forth as a thousand suns with an energy that tears apart, cuts asunder the stronghold of the Shadow. It reinstates the soul to Godhood, albeit by its own willing efforts.

"Ye hold the Key to Cosmic Power, Cosmic Lands, Cosmic Thought for ye are the power, the thought manifest, that can dart out into the Reaches of Cosmic Altitudes at will. The keeper of secrets enters, retreats, to Temples of gleaming Light, ye shall soon rise to the occasion more wakefully as ye walk in His Way, behold the Glories His Hand has wrought, would He only prove it to saints and withhold it from thee? I say not. I desire ye would forsake vanity that fritters away precious time, cleave to the Light, Beloved, that through inner renewal outer perfection may manifest. Be not as stragglers and drifters who fade into desparity and are like the dead to awaken no more, who linger under the shade-tree of Cosmos waiting for a new resurrection. Ye know the Way, walk in it!

"To live a life brave and clean in the spirit of detachment, is the precision tool that cuts away the brushwood of carnal being and cleans the mind of distortions. When stargazers say the constellation is wrong for thy worthy endeavors, how can it be wrong when He holds the Reigns? Ye need none other for there is none beside Him and He alone brings the soul into its Great Experience, when it obeys and yields to the precepts of regeneration and transformation. I thank thee."

I AM IN CHRIST
—A GUARDIAN OF TRANSFORMATION—

Ye Know the Way of the Will

"To All In Quest Of the *ONE;*

"I AM, Gabriel, in quest of truth you have come into My Light and this is My Counsel to the children upon earth: Keep open the Gates to Liberation, ye know the way that leadeth to Eternal Life and that which plummets to destruction. Soon the day cometh when all you fervently love, desired and clung to shall drop into faint recalling. All things of earth are but slender ties that shall utterly dissolve and perish, but virtue and freedom of soul shall follow into eternity. You take with you the energy of loving, giving, sharing, in the living atom and all the personality brought forth in the energy of unworthy deeds. If ye declare to love God, consider what ye despise, He is all things and within all. You claim hold of personal power? Consider your helplessness in dire distress.

"Keep vigil for the intensity of new Dispensations that shall pour forth into your world when the Angel loosens the Sixth Seal. He who has ears, let him hear! It is of Old Truth, heretofore only given to a few, for only few were ready. It shall prepare the soul for the hour when our Dispensations shall come to a close, as they are already silenced to the deafened ear of thy brethrens who in the good will of ecclesiology refute Cosmic Mandates and brought the children of God into bondage. Clear cut directions come to the seeker of God, the altars of earth shall crumble to ashes as some already have. By the Magnitude of the Great Dispensator souls shall be gathered up and some left behind, but among the chaff the golden wheat shall be found, souls that shall survive into the Golden Age and the New Dawn that is already upon you even now.

"You know the Way! Let none guide the soul but Him Who called it into His purpose. The carnal tongue defies all reason, wags, meddles into the affairs of others, robs the good fellow of his psychic space, while some of you kick up your heels in dens of doom and inquity and drugged into oblivion you claim a little uncouthness might add variety and spice to the labors of the Cosmic Plough! You cannot serve God and Bahl! It is the mirage of the tempest that leadeth into a great snare, filled with sorrow and weeping, God is not mocked! Lest ye feel the pangs of the medieval torture rack that pulls the soul into diverse directions, through indecision and swashbuckling faith. Ye know the Way, walk in it!

"How can the children of God hear the Clarion Call of Spirit when the mind is filled with the dull drum of worldly rock that awakens lowest passions in souls' holy centers and stops up the ear to hear the Music of the Spheres? Continuous struggle is not of Eternal Brightness of Cosmos. Ye bemoan thy cross, how can ye be nailed to it when ye know the way by which to become free? Some of you have become unbending and stiff-necked to the Will of God and must again regrant and regain the relaxed state of contentment.

"Your earth-brethren who are embittered by suffering know not the Law that governs Life. I say, all is effect to human causation. The downpull of grieving cannot affect the soul that is stationed in Him Who is the Way and the Life. Counsel him in truth, him, who calls his Creator merciless, say: unpleasantness as good rise from ones center, that he himself is the creator of his condition, and say: by Mercy's Hand he may be loosed. For such a one labored through many existences, failed to look for redemption within himself. I say, through painful demise, tried in the fires of the self, he becometh the Light-Bearer of tomorrow and shall pour the Water-Pitcher the Angel hands him upon the heads, hearts and parched lips of others that cry out for liberation.

"When the self is kept out of harm's way and confusion, fearful shivers and ensnarements shall be of past. Our Message to the Children of earth remaineth the same: 'Come ye apart' Beloved, fill thy cups at the Wellsprings of Life, take heart, take drink, that Love would fill thy earthen vessels with His Treasure. Walk honest, upright and nobly, ye are of Royalty and High Esteem.

"I say, *ENOUGH,* away with vexation, away with plagiarisms that steal away and altar Truth. By Rose and Cross it shall be no more, His Righteousness shall grant victory! Beloved of Christ, draw unto Him that governs thy direction. Hearken to the Spirit of God that shall baptize the soul in the Celebration of Eternal Mass; and a new Melody shall sing across the Harpstrings of the Sacred Soul and the candle lit shall shine brighter than a thousand suns and the Light thereof blot out all darkness. In that ye shall know ye are the Light of the world that streams out and runs back into the Heart of God.

"I now retreat but for a little while, I shall overshadow thee, each and all and grant protection; until ye step beyond Inner Portals into sunlit Worlds of Love, Liberty and Freedom and I shall meet thee face to face.

"I leave with thee a *PEACE, PEACE, PEACE,* I thank thee."

In the Whiteness of Eternal Light
I AM
—GABRIEL—

Force of the Atom

"To those who seek understanding I say, Hail! I AM KARIM, servant of the Lord. *I AM* come to fill the cup of hope if ye would clasp My hand that we may bridge the chasm from unbelief to knowingness.

"Ye behold light-forms of saints because ye are attuned to them, while it is vital to bring forth the benefit of communications, it is equally important that ye forsake the death-rattle of false doctrines, that offer the scrambles of a dead alphabet for bread that was baked in the ovens of man's unclean fancy! Remember O Seeker, the Word of the Lord: 'the letter killeth but the Spirit giveth life.' I counsel that ye would terminate outer search and retreat to the Upper Room where He promised to meet thee, teach thee all things that give wisdom to the dynamic soul, that would listen to the Sound of Inner Being, to the moving, rolling Melody of the Lifestream of Creation.

"Within and beyond the light frequencies of thine finer flesh operates the Grand Force of Energy that is life to every form. Cosmic Power is the movement ye feel in modified force and form, that spurs on or holds back. How ye govern it determines thy progress or regression, but is left to thine own discernment to do as ye wish. The Force stirs into action the functions of the lesser self, adds impetus to vibrations ye have set into motion. The thought-and-motor energy ye feed into they light-bodies and atomic systems are living intelligences, as is Divine Intelligence that guides thy footpath. It *is* Super-human Power. Ye cannot deny it, refuse it, ignore it, nor close thine eyes to it, nor turn from it, for it is rooted within thee as Lifestream from whence it issues forth to regenerate and do its own bidding. This flow of incandescent *ENERGY* moves through thine electronic light-forms as it also flows through any system in any world and universe of ITS Body. It plays through the mantle of its lesser Light, the Soul, and endeavors to bring holiness to every cell, fiber and atom thereof.

"External and internal, ye feel it likened to a fine spray of electricity, a soft, static energy that magnetizes or repels, thus the electro-magnetic force-field of every body, of every living cell, atom, fiber in any molecular structure is refurbished by its Benevolence, by which it is recharged, mayhaps depleted! It proves to him who seeks self-willed exit from his earthy estate a futile attempt. He, *SOUL,* liveth forever, soul is energy and Energy is *GOD,* how can ye destroy the indestructible?

"Man condemns himself by the life he lives, he ignores the restraints of Spirit. When it delivereth him, he feels robbed of his freedom under the cravings of his insurrections and vice and the battle is waged, until he becomes cognizant of the stern Law that governs him and grows law-abiding, content, productive, and rich. In such a one ye clearly perceive a transformation of color-spectrums in the finer self that grow in clarity and brilliance as he continues to abide in the Law. If ye behold evil within another, proudly saying ye rose to a loftier estate, ask thyself: am I that deceiver, that biggot, thief, maligner, pervert? Or am I the beast in the field or tree in the forest? Lo, ye are all of these, consciousness high or low cannot be dissected. And ask thyself: am I these by force, imposition, neglect, lust, control or degree? And ye shall discover how far ye emerged out of the carnal estate, and into spiritual being.

"And if thy findings please thee, say: A small particle of a Mighty Cosmos *I AM,* a grain of sand at the rim of a Mighty Sea, that glistens as the golden ray I AM that fell out of the Sun-Self of the God-Soul, redeemed by Its Current. And in thy transformation when ye enter Fairer Shores, ye shall no longer find a separation between God and thyself.

"Ye are Cosmos, all of Cosmos is within thee as ye enter through the Inner Gate. In lower worlds ye beautify cosmic structure or temporarily destroy part of it in form, but the essence as it were recreates itself in new manifestations for it is the Force, the Life of all. When ye think, ye create. In God-Worlds ye create even better for the energy current is not ensnared as in lower worlds and of greater magnitude. Over There ye build thy homes by thought, the purer thy mental patterns, the finer is the garment ye shall wear. Impersonal Love must pattern the seamless robe, every stand and weave of the light-garment, else thine own creations shall turn on thee in reverberation of misused energy that assail body and mind with dis-ease. The solar and planetary Scanner examine each force-field, registers the slightest change in the electronic energy-equilibrium, therefore let man forsake his unholy rites and build towards perfection! What ye sow ye reap!

"Beloved, behold thyself pure to be pure, let none but the highest move thine deepest intents and ye shall have a clear perception and vision of the unlimited Self and soar free as birds in the sky to Yonder Worlds. Be not wise in conceit, but wise in discernment. Ask thyself: what have I now that rules my principles? Is it a force of good or otherwise? Do I mirror an honorable personage or one contrite, aggressive and haughty that obscures the Light veiled by egotistic notions! If ye turn from goodness, be not dissatisfied if thy own misery findeth thee. Be not as those who ask for Grace who never honored their last commitment! There is nothing as profitable to the soul as *INSTRUCTIONS,* for what can be more agreeable than the felicity of a wholesome life! Beloved, treat not with those who rule falsely, whose subjects listen but despise them, for their vexed paths shall culminate in sorrow.

"In thy goodly intentions when ye realize thou art nothing and God is All, ye finally have the concept of what the personality is and can depict between carnal nature and that which is Divine. Ye are but a single note in a Grand Cosmic Orchestra, that descended to earth on its Melody and shall bear thee up again and again until ye are Gods.

"I spoke to thee from the deep Center of Light and would ye might pray: '*LORD, O* increase my love for Thee, so that I may serve Thee better from day to day.'"

IN THE LIGHT OF TRANSFORMATION
I AM
—KARIM—

Chapter Seven

Instructions on Wholeness

When in God-centeredness we turn to our inner life for directions, we find the Angel does not give a Dialogue, but speaks short and to the point. You will seldom hear more than one sentence, two at most. In Divine Interchange thought answers to thought. Angelic Forces drop a melodic note into the questioning mind, by which the listener perceives the meaning of what is being said. In transmutation this manifests a correlation of words to him and sentences which of course are more at length than the original inflection. Dialogues with Masters and Dispensations from other Divine Regents flow through heart and pen like pearls running down a conveyor belt in such quick succession that unless you use short-hand or deliver the Message directly to others you may lose half of the context.

To encounter the Holy Presence of an Angel is a great Benediction. We feel enveloped by a wonderful Presence as though God Himself were in the room with us, Angelic Rays flood the whole being with penetrating warmth and leave with us a Love that lingers on for many days, even months. Whether we are attuned to them or not, in this small space of time our perception grows keenly alert. We think we see them externally but it is rather our inner perception that grants us to behold their radiant Presences. They appear to believers and unbelievers alike when the need of the hour calls for their aid. Suddenly we know how to solve a problem and at times an incurable illness has vanished as wordless conversation takes place.

The power of God's Divine Regents is immense but gentle, and man's scoffing does not diminish their Glory. Many wonder how they might know if it is the Angel or a sinister force, knowing the latter can appear in various garbs and guise. We may be sure the Angel will not draw into our vibrations unless our life is rooted in Christ, anchored in spiritual living or proves good morality. A specter would rather be drawn to vice than virtue and only appeared on the mental screen or in another guise to satisfy various notions and the five passions of the flesh; whereas the Angel comes to fulfill the Purposes of the Lord.

When the benedictions of Angelic Light permeate our auric force-field it also fortifies us inwardly and forms a powerful protective shield around us. The more we yield to a virtuous life the clearer we shall perceive the Angel. We may be sure that even those who do not pray are loved and cared for by the selfless servers of the Angelic Kingdom.

There are times when the Guardian counsels us in matters of proper nutrition, it is just as important to care for the body as it is for our inner being, every aspect of man must come into the fullness of God-Harmony. The thoughts on health that you believe to be your own are in reality divine insights given by the Angel. Those who do not heed or perhaps cannot hear the Inner Voice, the Angel will contact during the dreamstate either in the form of a decisive Voice or by the actual appearance of a Being of Light. This conversation will remain vividly in the dreamer's mind upon awakening. The dream state and Dream World are the continuation of our day. Life goes on just the same for consciousness never sleeps proving there is action in inaction. Those who say they never dream, have only a block in creativity either through persistent problems or too much rejoicing in worldly activities that take no thought of God.

Without intent to inject fear it must be mentioned that the Holy Presence of an Angel can be overwhelming in that our lesser being can at times barely endure their pristine frequencies; it can make you tremble like a tender leaf. God bless the day when we can become more like them and behold their Reality more clearly.

Our spiritual practice embraces persons from all walks of life, seekers that come for help. Yet only the Help from within aids them, we are but the vessel. The following are spontaneous answers received for the petitioner.

This was given to a person in fear of fainting and it said:
"BRING THINE EMOTIONS UNDER CONTROL, FEAR NOT THE SILENCE."

To one experiencing trying conditions:
"I AM ST. GERMAIN, I WILL HELP THEE."

To a struggling dieter:
"USE THY WILL, NOT THE PILL, I SHALL COUNSEL THEE!" in consequence the person lost eighteen pounds in two weeks.

About death:
"BELOVED, FEAR NOT DEATH FOR IT IS LIFE."

About smoking:
"POLLUTE NOT THE BREATH OF GOD, WHAT IS THERE THAT YE LOVE MORE?"

Once I questioned the use of a tea and He answered:
"DRINK THAT TEA, IT IS WELL FOR THEE, HERBS ARE TREASURES OF NATURE."

About Life:
"LOVE, LIVE AND BE HAPPY, THAT HAPPINESS FROM FAIRER SHORES MAY FIND THEE."

About confusion:
"IT IS PART OF THINE EXPERIENCE, A LESSON TO BE LEARNED."

—Saint Germain—

Conversations with this Counselor are always very short. His helpfulness comes to us at the spur of the moment. While on tour, a woman called me to help her husband who had suffered severe burns on the foot, which had not healed after six months of medical treatment. What to do? I attuned myself to Spirit. While she was still on the phone, the Celestial Herbalist gave a remedy, instructing the use of a combination of herbs and drops of natural oils to be pressed into a poultice and applied to the foot. She immediately followed suggestions and after three days the large, aching wound had closed and healed without redness or a trace of scarring and the excruciating pains left only moments after the first applications. Over the years I have seen the wonder-working power of Etheric Remedies take effect many times, these worked for me as well. It is when mortal knowledge has no answer and also at other times, that Higher Forces bring the body back into harmony and restore us. It proves the Great unseen is our reality and true help.

Celestial Instructors are not merely concerned with physical and spiritual healing, but most importantly they will show us how to remove the *CAUSE* that induced the effect to our suffering. When I asked to be shown how I could revitalize my energies, the Physician of the Healthy Way replied:

"*I AM* come to instruct, health shall blossom when you sever connections from undesirable contacts. Look situations square in the eye, see them for what they are and walk away. Do not give in to the pitiful pleas of those who would rend' thee again; when you ease their burden it becomes your own. Such associations rob the body of vitality, no matter how well the intent. Dust away the germs of negation, let them be swept up and swept out to clear the mind, too much altruism serves no one.

"Then sit under the Sun-Light of Spirit, turn the face of the soul upward like a flower to the sun, absorb its rays into the self, into the body, into your bones, blood and nervous-system by intent and see it wash away the dross leaving the body through the soles of the feet. Then new strength shall flood all systems and flush away all else. Do you understand?

"Here is what you take to fortify the flesh: In the morning you shall partake of one glass of tepid water drawn from the spring, place therein the juice of one-quarter lemon, one-quarter of honey, let misture dissolve, drink lukewarm. The body needs small quantities of foodstuff, one does not feed the body, but the blood. Take dessicated liver each morning, noon and night in small quantity for nine days. The body before us shall partake of the marrow of calcium upon arising, at noon and night for nine days. Drink one glass of tea made of leaves of the comfrey bush at night, this will soothe the intestines. Do so for nine days. Energy shall then be at a maximum (if suggestion is followed as directed).

"We watch over soul's conditions, we teach the Way to Health. Attune yourselves!

"Blessings, Flowers, Joy and *LOVE!*"

Devotedly I AM,
—SIGAMATRA—

Heavenly remedies are not medical suggestions, though they have worked for me for a lifetime, they might not work for another. I remember when a bottle of cider vinegar fell on my foot and split it open, immediately the Voice instructed I should pour a small amount of it over the open wound. I did so, with tongue in cheek and jumped a mile by the sting, but the wound closed before my eyes and left neither bruise or soreness.

Why Am I Dizzy?

It became evident that a Magnificent Force attended our healing work, stacks of mail attested to the fact, there was no end to joyful letters of gratuity. Among other requests was a letter from a person who expressed considerable concern over repeated dizziness that could not be medically diagnosed or remedied. As I read on, I felt a heat and the healing petition in my hand began to vibrate with energy, and almost like a light-ray called down from heaven the Master's Voice spoke in reply:

"The imbalance of the body before us is not rooted in physical cause but in the spiritual aspect. The soul induced a process of regeneration by which stronger light bodies are being built. Thus, this body is experiencing a slight imbalance and at times slight breathing discomforts which shall pass. We here see the outer form shall be a more effective vehicle to carry out a mission and a task after body and soul are again in proper alignment with Spirit. The inner being shall then be able to gather much valued information from Higher Consciousness for the good of others. There is no cause for concern, all is well, be at peace."

Needless to say the person was restored to perfect balance thereafter, as the thankful answer was soon received.

Having myself experienced similar discomforts, the Spirit gave counsel, saying:

"Motion in Nimbus now square to receive Messages and Dictations. Soul must relinquish self-will and carry out instructions as We have given. The carnal nature created a tug of war in indecision of whether to obey, or stay in the dregs of materialism, whereby frictions and imbalance added to more discomforts than has been said. Ye must be stabilized to carry out a mission to help others, forget pride, outward help must be accepted as He helps through others to aid thy cause. A foundation of strength and confidence must be layed in Him to receive the Teachings of Rare Truth. Let the Holy Comforter ever guide! This body is in fine condition, must now proceed as planned. Guidance is secured, destination charted by us. Albeit, the Monad of form is in present expansion, discomforts shall vanish. Be at peace!"

I AM IN CHRIST
—A BODHISATTVA—

It was sure I became better fast and soon left home and hearth in exchange for a life of serving others. It behooves us to see so much suffering in the world and when I ponder upon these, sometimes an Angel-Voice of Comfort speaks up:

"You must learn to discern between the matter of material substance and the matters of God, these must work in balance. When the physical body is out of kilter its emotional part soon follows. We would that you may stand rooted in the Love of God as strong as the oak and not be the willow that bends in the storm and weepeth—. And We say, balance must be that suffering may end. As you eat the Manna of Heaven you must also eat the bread of man, keep balance! For only in balance can you cross safely the bridge to Higher Consciousness. Let no wearisome person disturb your peace, be not afraid, but do what is proper and do it quickly, ever curbing and subduing the destructive elements that are. Take on the mantle of golden-white peace, dedicate the best you have to each and everyone and Love and Hope shall ever flame before thee as a celestial lantern and shine into the darkest hour of the heart.

"In tender-hearted mercy, do not bemourn the suffering of any, for painful conditions allow for regrouping of thoughts that in surrender of a self-ruled life it would also bring victory over painful conditions. Then, by the mere Touch of His Hand those who are at war with their own thoughts, with their own selves, shall drop their weapons and no longer hold their rendezvous with death, but behold a more beautiful dawning. My Child, there are those who neither feel, see nor hear the things of God, only in illness do they behold the Christ, for they are the Christ of their own cross. Sorrow and discomforts are Golden Rays that wash the soul by its own tears. May it be recognized that even in suffering a true blessing is found.

"Illness does not defeat God's Plan for the humble soul, though it may leave it with a blessing or a scar, for sharp edged trials are the instrument of testing Love.

"Be silent, prayerful, rejoice! In utter acceptance of Divine Intervention no matter how unacceptable it may seem, there will be sunshine and a Sacred Eucharist for meat and a Light for a drink, these shall restore the being to wholeness and bring it to *LOVE.*"

IN THE LIGHT OF WISDOM
I AM
—AN ANGEL OF LOVE—

Take Dominion and Be Healed

"To all Who would hear!

"Children of the Flaming Light, as I have spoken to the hearts of man, woman and child throughout the Ages, I, SINGH DE LURE, Guardian of the Fires of Purity, speak to you from the High Courts of God to give My Dispensation through the Scribe.

"The immense quest of regeneration that releases the soul from carnal ways into Christ-Purity seems not the be for everyone. But to those who unafraid set foot upon the narrow way of purification it shall become clear, the subservient Spirit is the *ONLY* Link and very Life to which each soul must gravitate to avoid the fate of regression. Regression and transmigration is a bitter drink to those who disbelieve in re-embodiment, but His Law is unchangeable, what ye sow ye reap, reform must be. Some possess the cruelty of animals and treat His little ones in grueling fashion in laboratories to feed man's vanity, torture them in common place and common ways, verily, as ye done it unto them ye done it unto Him. What you are you become whether animal or angel by your good choice, that is Nature. Regeneration to Godhood or regression to lesser form is Nature also. You can only reap the fruits of your own actions, which shall it be? As you regress to a lower form in self-undoing, would the monad of the creature be denied a higher state by its own good merits and evolution? A cold awakening does induce a more humble state of mind, albeit the children of earth do not wish to hear the truth We dispense!

"Many of you living in the physical-material world rush about to expand your scope of materialism by which to drown out discontent, lack and fear, yet beneath and beyond your drives, ruthless ambitions and riveting speeches lies the deep need to know the Lord of your body, He is expressing Himself as *YOU* and this omnipotent Force within you stirs you to move into various directions that confusion may bring you back to realize Him! The lights of incarnate consciousness come into our Presence, some pure, others weakly malignant. If ye would take dominion over every destructive habit, ye would be healed momentarily and permanently. But we will not impose nor penetrate the dense veil of human vibrations when you shut the door to light and continue frolicking in the ways of iniquity. You have expression of free will. The purity, strength, chastity, and peace of Natural Law that once was dropped into the cradle of every heart is diminishing, the darkness of Assure has snatched it up, defiled it in the dregs of degeneration, and this with man's own consent. Know ye not, negation can only corrupt through your own thoughts and actions? 'Woe be unto thee Assure who hidest the unrighteous in thee!' And even as we forewarn and instruct, it meets with a deaf ear, humanity refuses the Voice.

"If the Shadow is not at work why do we see sorrow, lack, depletion of energy and plagues betide the bodies of men? It is because souls upon earth have become hypnotized by the gold of Mammon, have denied the Gold of God and exchanged the crowning glory of joy and contentment for the illusions of trinkets and brass that belong to the physical-material world. As Persephone it has wandered off too far from the House of the Father and so it must live under the influence of the forces of Hades until it repaid its debt to the tinsel of demagogues, albeit it would consent to live a sanctified life, it cannot be otherwise.

"We are waiting for your call, Beloved of the Light, to be permitted to help in the exchange of your lesser attributes for the Divine Attributes of God. 'Who then shall open the windows of heaven and pour out blesings, that there shall be no room to receive it!' And we know the time shall come to everyone when outer needs can no longer fill your inner void, when inner emptiness shall yawn as the bottomless pit where the mind feels and hears the weeping and gnashing of teeth within itself. Children of earth, it is then that the strong are made weak and the weak become strong and many shall run in fear from one earth physician to another only to end up drugged into greater confusions. It is never because the physician has failed his patient, but because the latter failed himself by closing the door to the only Source that can restore him to wholeness either through the physician, or a channel, or directly through himself. Illness is lack of spiritual Grace, a state induced by misqualifications of energies, a state of mind. Only the Light of the Sun-Self can overcome the weakness of its lesser part and nurture it back by the way of spiritual living.

"We see persons on earth who maliciously turn ill health to their advantage, some devote their lives to being a patient. This only adds to their next existence the Karmic condition of insecurity, heavy responsibilities by that they learn self-reliance no matter what the cost and come to know the *INNKEEPER* upon Whom their very welfare depends. Many a soul has been saved by self-improvement!

"One who super-imposed his will upon others leaning on the props of illness and who endeavored to secure his comfort by seeking to strip his helpers of their self-identity, making of them a chattel; when he is layed to rest his hatefulness still plays across the face and soon he entereth a corresponding estate more sorrowful than the last.

"Shall we now begin to cure the ills of carnality to bring the soul back into its own divinity and wholeness? Let virtue be your steady companion, soften the hardened heart, abstain from deadly gossip and infernal match making, purify your thoughts, your actions, abstain from all manner of evil and walk not in the path of the ungodly. Endeavor to align the self to every positive force and come into His Audible Silence, in your light-form you shall realize your conscious connection with God. Keep the mind in lofty detachment and the Soul ever in Him, Who is the Life, the Light and the Way.

"The scripture speaketh of death, of harmful habits in which the humble wayfarer indulges himself with no thought of soul or God; but death is meant no otherwise than death to lust, self-hate, envy, greed, malice, vicious maligning, anger, attachment, pride, and trickery of all sorts, that brings death to the material entity. Until you forsake the self-ruled path of the spiritually dead you cannot enter your transformation in Christ. And so you continue in endless rounds of reincarnation, life after life, death after death until you drop all and come into His Light—the naked soul, receiving the crown He alone can give in the freedom of Total awareness. For in Him ye have Eternal joy, Eternal Life and it stands written: 'God made no death, neither has He pleasure in the destruction of the living...for He knoweth how to deliver the goodly out of temptation...but chiefly them that walk after the flesh in lust of uncleanness, and despise government.'... We say, be ye wise, for the golden kernel of soul endureth the waiting at the threshold and the chaff falleth back upon the dung-heap of corruption. This is why few follow the Light and those who lose patience are governed by their instincts of survival that forsake them in the end. The Way seemeth too hard, the light of materialism obscures the Vision of God. But in his search of Him man giveth up nothing, neither does he gain, since all he needs and desires are already his, for he is the Light unto himself and can bring forth all he wishes by command.

"And when you come to Him in Silence, omit the strain of being bent into a pretzel or the envisioning of useless symbols, but let the soul flow with the Vision to take on the radiant Garment of the Lord.

"We thank you for partaking of Our Teachings. I stand at the Gate of Consciousness holding the Torch of the Flame of Purity that illumines the Pathways of Freedom."

I AM—IN CHRIST—
—SINGH DE LURE—

Chapter Eight

Heavenly Highways of Servitude

"And it shall come to pass in the last days, saith God, I will pour my spirit upon all flesh; and your sons and daughters shall prophesy, and your young men shall have visions, and your old men dream dreams. And on my servants and on my handmaidens I will pour out into those days my spirit; and they shall prophesy." (Acts 2-17:18)

The "Calling" is not for one or two, but in time the Thunder and Light of the Inner Voice shall zig-zag across every inner horizon, streak through the darkness of every personality and crack the shell of hardened attitudes, piety and pride. All shall hear the Bells of Love and Gongs of Freedom that calls souls into service. And then perhaps some of us might feel at loss as how to start and where, but soon we realize that service begins at ones own center, that it must first manifest within if it would ray out to benefit the whole. Self-realization brings us to understand others better and it is not self-satisfying love but self-appreciation that grants deeper insights in which lies our Eternal Hope.

Governing Masters and Angels direct us until we have met with the qualification to become Their helpers and They aid us further in the attainment of Adeptship and Masterhood Consciousness.

The Messages to follow are helpful to those who have heard the "Call" and to others who stand in the wings in readiness to set foot upon Heavenly Highways of servitude. And though a message may take on a personal aura, it shall shed its light of consolation into many hearts and upon every footpath.

Divine Regents who instruct us in the Way, remove our sense of struggle and point to the bright shining of the Rose of Attainment that beckons to us from the finishing point.

If Ye Would Serve

"To All Who would follow the Call;

"You have come to hear My Counsel! I see some of you have brought your luggage to begin your travels into the planes of service, but it is better to travel light and to leave the material bundle behind, if you would work unencumbered!

"Once you have begun to till the ground, forsake not the plough, you cannot do so without pain, for the rains pour down and wash away goodly seeds and you must plough a new furrow and sow a new seed. Whether your chores are in the fields, in mothering and fathering the family, whether in factory or public place or as Handmaiden of God, it matters not! But how you serve determines the blessing, is it willingness or shun? In your labors look not to God for what He can give, but love Him for what He is, as even He loves the soul as Himself. And when ye utter ye love Him, He quickly uttereth back: 'If ye love me, keep My Comandments!' Thus, beginning thy service ye may prove what ye love and how well. And hide not the baggage of worldliness behind your back for 'ye cannot serve two masters!'

"The fulfillment of a mission requires demonstration of courage, fortitude and honesty and to labor with a sense of system and order, to fulfill every duty in the gladness of a happy heart, whether in prayer, supplication, washing utensils, caring for the sick, or giving a sermon, let each be a gift to God, let it be done in His Name that you may have nothing to reproach yourself for, nor suffer drudgery.

"And when your hands are cupped to receive His blessing, know that help cometh not before time, but in the hour of need and ask not to receive any good until you have given it yourself. Ask not your good to come out of another's pocket but from Him Who giveth the increase. Beloved servers of the Christ-Cause, I recruit and counsel you to serve in a goodly way that you may prosper. Be not weary of the mocker that attempts to trample the joy who stealeth thy pleasures of God-Intent, for you shall rise again in many forms to bear witness to Love. Fear not the arrow darting from the mouth of the wicked, nor deceits piercing thy side, for you endure so in remembrance of the Humble Fisherman Who loved thee in Kingship, Who seeth the things that are, Who shall polish thy light to crystal brightness and sancitfy thee.

"And though your light be a mixture of laughter and tears,

as sunshine and rain mingled to a beautiful rainbow, it shall affirm your Covenant with God and manifest His Promise to you. And as you gather up the coins of Love strewn along the barren terrains of earth and along the steep, winding trails that lead to God, you shall indeed be rich. I say to the Scribe and to all Light-Bearers who would serve: treat not with him who is caught up in his own world, who would entice thee to forsake heavenly pathways, but bring thy tokens of concrete faith and unwavering commitment to the Altar of God, and He shall give His Bounty when you least expect, for, what you gave in grace returneth by Grace an hundred-fold. Tremble not in fear to venture into new pastures, for the Hallow of His Hand shall cover thee, and We, the Guardians shall grant thy victory in each just fight.

"Be not dismayed, O Children of Grace, when stronger light-bodies are being built, causing weakness and oft' great physical discomforts, for as He disassembles the finer self He shall reassemble it to glorious perfection and know what is given out of necessity shall pass. Let not your garments bear stains of doubt.

"When you keep calm and pure and forsake the laws of Mammon that appease carnal appetites, darkness shall not hinder your noble task. I send you into the dregs of Bahl that your loving, serving and giving in discernment would warm the hearts of men and break the chains of corruption by the power of the Valiant Light. And if your pathways lead through the fiery baptism of the self, know that while you serve you work off the karma brought into this life, for serving Him does not obliterate the debt you owe. Hold fast to the plough, ye were bought with a price and must step through the Refiner's Fire to bring forth the gold for the ransom of others.

"If you would serve the Living God, be a brave warrior and when the yoke bears heavy on your shoulders it is because you bear the yoke of all, serving Christ Who beareth it within thee. And I say, heavy it is, for man upon earth jumpeth from one ill response into another. He gives way to uncontrolled anger and in judicial arrogance robs his companions of holy birth-right and the mother of her child, commits treason against himself and his God. He does not realize his heritage to Divine Estate nor does he care. And now the children of God are assigned to clean up the outer path of their brethren, that the latter would see the

Flame of Love amidst the maze of confusion and find redemption. It is said, ye shall do without doing—wipe clean the mind of folly, for how can ye do without doing less ye let His Love flow through thy works and thyself *that* calleth for *ACTION* and not relinquishment of service, as the false teacher would command while he himself goes into action and depriveth others of rendering their works to God.

"Be faithful, valiant and true to His Command, forge ahead to break the chains of bondage within yourself and the whole. Be steadfast if ye would serve the Christ!"

DEVOTEDLY I AM
—A WATCHER OF THE WAY—

Dialogue with an Angel of St. Michael

There came a time when I wanted to forget it all. Sickness, weakness and want came out of nowhere. After many years of service I even doubted that I had a mission. It was never easy and I gladly endured in face of the many blessings God manifested to others. But it seemed enough was enough, inharmony and more grief reared its ugly head and in view of the happiness I saw all around, surely, I thought, I must be on the wrong path. The nights of soul were very dark, in fact, it was more of living in a catacomb from which there seemed no other way out but to hang it all on the nail. Since Masters get tired of their crying disciples I waited until I was really ready to throw in the towel before asking Their Help and just a little more would finally move my decision over the edge. And then came the Voice, oh yes, an Angel of the Legions of Saint Michael that moved me back into the Way. The Shining Being had the kindest eyes I had ever seen and His Words and sentences droppped as balm into my weary heart:

"You doubt you have a mission? You doubt there is a God, a heaven, a hell? If so, everyone could do as he pleased and your world would turn into a blood-bath! And I say, there is much in your world that you must make commitment to again! A part of you rushed into the world of want that part must be removed, that there can be the part of Grace given again.

"*I AM* a part of your creation, a part of knowledge that is, that you must attain. Because you have wronged, you must learn now to regrant by supplication, before We, the Angels will speak of your work. You must again make the commitment vow you had given long before. Your world, it is not because you have angered it, but your world has created an illusion of power and greed, not of you, Child, but what is committed to you by *OTHERS'* acts of want and desire.

"You came into this world a gifted one and this you shall always remain. You know this from your time of others who have received that bounty of charm, as Michael will send His Angels only to those who have given their grace to God. You have done so all your life and now within your time of weakness you are brought to supplication. It is not a moment of sadness, Child, it is a moment of knowing your Grace. You have chosen the vesselship of where all Light of pure Christ-Tears will pour within your being and enter every cavity of your existence. Much of your need will always be met, but that is your Grace, but to give forth its honor you must now in your own time bring service back to your heart. Then, and only then, will WE be allowed through the veil to clasp between you the Sacred Order and the knowledge of the material world.

"These things are honored to those who seek. We cannot speak of things you are to do, but We can tell you, that, that which you are to do has always been great, shall be great. But know you are the instrument, the Divine Channel, the Giving Grace. No longer speak of I, but of We, the Angels. No longer speak in terms of possessions, but in terms of release.

"Those you have been taught, that now the weaker part is given this veil...and put before you such demands, that you had weakened. Now in your weakness you are seeking Light. Again you will make supplication and each one that you make is greater than the last. This Chalice is poured upon the heart so that you may feel—and to feel this energy is the gift you always had, but have lost some of its touch, only because the world of pressure and desire came in and veiled you. And there for a time you forgotten to draw your sword and slice away its grip. Now the Sword is handed back to you and when it is truly pure and the strength of your supplication is made, you go forward to heal those in Love that you have always felt, you then will honor.

"You will not touch the material world for your needs, you will walk and know, as poverty is poverty, strength is strength, these cannot change. An individual is married to Christ when they give to that which they have been taught. And you have brought much with you from Childhood and you will bear it forever! In that, you cannot turn away, you can only go forward. We give you consolation by knowing We shall stand beside you. We give you consolation in knowing it will be YOUR supplication."

I asked: "What is supplication?"

The Angel replied: "Supplication means a gift to God, in this you will give up into your thoughts and prayers—you must give something away each time. You make twelve supplications, twelve gifts. Then choose the vow of poverty, that, you may carry with you. All that you earn goes into a Foundation or some place where it can be used. We, the Angels, come to you from Michael. We are preparing you, since We are from Michael, for a new Order in your life, which is not easy for you, but is something within yourself you know you must do. There will be many obstacles confronting you before it is done, this is only to make you aware of the completion, that you have purged everything.

"With all things, God will provide, and it is in this time that the world is filled with greed and materialism, there must be those who walk without greed. They must walk without the means that other men *MUST* have. This you have given, but have not been comforted by, and now you must give comfort and seek what is provided for you. Use what is necessary to feed soul and body, but all other is to be put for the use of the work you will do. The caring, the helping, the writing of books, the speaking of tapes that you send to others, that they may hear the strength and power given, that they may understand the Light of God's Wisdom.

"Whatever is provided momentarily for them to send you, is put back into the work, a constant inpouring until there are others that follow and bring their light to show they may do the same. That they may grow and understand. This is what you have come into this world to do, this is what you shall do. And from your foundation all is poured into it there provided for you, but provided also a means for others to seek and bring their truth to a way of learning.

"You are taught by the Angels of God and through your mouth they do speak, and from what We speak through you will show others a greater power than they have known upon their world of material greed, jealousy and envy, for those are the things that weaken them and cause them pain."

I questioned: "Should I sell the house and rent a place?"

He answered: "Your foundation should be a place built within the country, from there correspondence reach out, in time it will be provided. You must never see yourself again on the road of life as you traveled far to aid the Christ-Cause, until that time is shown. You must wait for the signs and marking-stones in trust and faith. You are no longer weak, do not utter these words before us, We will not listen, nor will We turn our face to you if you do this. We will make you angered by the purge of your supplication, for this is the Law of God. Until you understand these Laws and quit crying out in anger and your needs, then you will learn these things of wrath, God's Anger is great, but His Mercy pure."

I questioned: "Why do I get so tired and weak giving counsel to persons over the telephone or in person?"

And the Angel of Michael replied: "Call upon the Lord of Gods, of Hosts, to bring in the Light within you and that will be your work, no other, no strength will be given if you are drained, lay and sleep in God's Hands. If you feel their pull, ask them to take all they need for themselves and to grow stronger by reaching up to Christ for the needs they have. In order for you to show greater service, the God of all Power permitted illness, through this you are able to write, communicate, and make people understand that even if their burden is heavy, that through it they may be healed. Because of your illness you become a great saint. A saint not recognized in your time, but long after you have left the flesh and gone to other Kingdoms.

"By being attacked, by being pierced, you know what it is to be through anguish that other persons in this world must suffer, because they have polluted, destroyed, they have hurt their own glory. You see and sense in their world that they have created. Through your sensing, your ability to know, the more you hold and come stronger, you understand why the Angel of the Morning is attacking you, that he has to be cared for also, because God created him.

"You are getting stronger, tho' you feel the weakness that other people out there in the world are crying about. Their pain is greater than you have to bear, but what you bear is great to you. You will eat no meat, you will eat only fruit, that is prepared by the seed of God, take only that into your being. Then from the tree of the Comfrey bush you will partake and brew it as an herb, bless it! You will put within it the Holy Spirit and see the dove and Eucharist become one. You will sense the Power of God within you and know you are fighting the battle for God's Children. This will be your true redemption to Heaven and the Chalice you must carry that others will be healed upon earth.

"This is your healer's happiness, your Light you must use. No one else has but a greater gift than yours, but it is a gift wrought with peril, for it must face all that is in darkness and it is this, that brings you into the Mastership and your completion. It is this that will make you angry with the Lord, but the Lord God, your Creator and His Heavenly Host has set you before men and women to show the Power of God is fulfilled. This will be your Truth, Wisdom and bring you into the Light and Kingdom of God. This work you must carry, let nothing else stir you from the path. Let no fear be your obstacle, if it is, walk stronger!"

I asked: "What can I do to dissipate the Shadow?"

"BLESS THEM!" answered the Angel. And then He continued in the Prayer of the Gods:

"O, Michael, My Great Eternal Protector, and Legions, Armies and Angels of God, I ask that thy red, flaming Sword come forth, and slay the Shadow back into the remnants of hell, that these may be purged and neither purge or touch my being, that these may not strengthen away the things I must do, I ask they are a thief in the night and be taken from me, I ask thee to be chained in hell and may not come forward again into my aid, for I am aided by God. I am aided by the Light and not by darkness, these things I pray."

"Where will my next chapel be?"

"Go within the country and find land when the time is appointed. It will show itself to you as you will see a white dove, and when it appears it will show you to follow."

"Will I leave my home state?"

"Yes, you will go East, We, the Angels protect and guide you, this is all for this day."

I STAND IN THE
LEGIONS OF MICHAEL—
I AM—AMAND—

This saving Message has always been close to my heart, even though all the rest were received in deep appreciation, for without it I might have given up. Many things have come to pass, some are yet to take place and so, the nearness and Realities of Angels is a certain stronghold and Instructions are sure to follow if we would perk up the ears of the soul and listen.

Gathering Forces

"Hail, Servants of the Light!

"Come, Beloved, come! Kneel before the Altar of Service. Take your torch and light it at the Flame of Freedom that soars high into Cosmic Dimensions magnetizing the downpouring of the Fires of Life to fill the hearts of men on earth in the Love and Light of Holy Conversation.

"A Mighty Cause calls workers of light into the Harvest-Field, to teach the way of devotion, to sow, to pluck up, and bring the Golden Wheat to the Cosmic Storehouse. Think not ye labor in vain or alone. Legions of Angels are looking over your shoulders to count the bushels and Hearken! The Master's Footfall is heard walking among His Workers.

"Now I say to the Scribe and to all, let us gather our forces and join the work laid before us, that that which shall come thereafter would produce a feast at the Table of the Lord! When you do and dare, the radiant Self gives consent, honors the work that channels upon earth may produce fruitfulness in every endeavor and material abundance would be but a fraction of your blessing.

"Hear Scribe, go and do His bidding for the hour has come to reach out, branch out, but home base is needed, flittering around from here to there, packing the bundle, living out of the vehicle? What manner of service is this? Know ye not He shall provide in all things? When faith falters, unrest follows, so does depletion of energies! We would you might be less concerned with the craving of the body and rather concentrate on that that would benefit others. You have come through trial and tribulation and only a mite better for the wear, but though you whimper, complain and cry, you know how to Love and it is because of Love that you now stand before the Maker ready to receive directions that must be carried out precisely and immaculately as is the Light.

"There shall be a place for you, where song-bird, wood and stream and bowers of greenery adorn the premise and it shall be as a religion you feel, that Spirit of Nature, unlike the weeping nostalgia of belief and creed. This place you know not of but it is prepared, that the lame, the blind, the downtrodden and the weary heart may come to unburden.

"Some of you have tired of honoring beliefs and traditions out of need to go in search of Self, but what is the Radiant Self if not Christ? In present weariness keep patience, for the Light shall dawn! In your labors and yearning to forge onward, wait upon Him Who knoweth what ye shall do and how it shall be done. Be not moved, wait in humbleness of heart as a child with the plate waiting to be served until a sure sign moves you onward; and a Light shall go before you and one shall follow while yet another shall overshadow and uphold. Faith and Hope are the Wings of Spirit that lift out of the valley of frustrations, lest you go off on counterpart tangents and join the plot where grass grows and whithers on the tomb of him whose unholy actions found no common ground with his professed belief. Having pledged the Self to service, the effects to non-compliance are less sympathetic than the retribution to him who erred all day.

"Beloved Servants of the Light, beware of the quackery of false teachers, self-sanctified they deny the Christ. They are not surrogates of the Light nor Its Emissaries, albeit they teach light by plagiarism. Their assurgent dialogues, repertoires, stoic teachings, and surreptitious literature are asymmetrical to Divine Law. They are Usurpers and *ASTRAL SEDUCERS* to the soul! Who give lithe, witty answers in guru-like fashion. In austere judgement of pseudo-mastership they admonish you not to see the Vision of God nor to feel the restoring Voltage of His Holy Spirit while in their psychic nature they do otherwise.

"Walk through their life and you shall find lack of good conduct, covered up immortality, lack of charity, self-exaltation and lack of Christ. They claim saviorship that would guide beyond death, believe them not! For in the end they are the Aspen that jitters by the Breath of God, Who shall not spare them for they are Anti-Christ. O, we would not deny them their lessons in the Law, but say, you who have found and live in the Imperial Majesty of Christ the Lord, be neither swayed nor blinded by their clever teachings. And We ask the true servant of Light to be assiduous in carrying out the work We shall place before one and all."

MAY LOVE AND INSPIRATION BE YOUR GUIDE
—I AM—A GUARDIAN OF THE CHRIST WAY—

The Way to Love and Perfection:

To reach the point of inner peace had been my desire for nearly a lifetime, finally it seemed to have come true. As worldly problems lost their grip on me I concluded the world was a beautiful place to live in, after all, and that peace would be mine as long as I kept the vision of the soul upon the Light and heard the Melody of God sing through my inner being. I lived in both worlds, if not in all. The knowingness and heavenly experience of God taught me that true spirituality makes its own quiet statement and often silence was golden, indeed, as balanced detachment became my way of life.

I no longer questioned my achievements, they were God's, not mine and except for following the call there was nothing left to be achieved. The more I learned to step aside, the more profoundly Divine Inflections found Its expression through me. The praise and adulation people lavished on me left me untouched and at times rather uncomfortable, for it belonged to Him Whom I loved, that wondrous, unspeakable IT that was the core of my very existence, the Giver of all life, all inspirations, fortitudes and fruits of every labor. But having come to God doesn't mean your life is suddenly made perfect! More often, karmic consequences are worked out right along with progress, to harrow out the residue of egocentric notions, to develop within us the Character of Christ that calls for faithfulness, courage, endurance, perfection and Love.

The cloak of night had spread its gentle filament of sleep over the world, the quietude of the hour moved me to muse and contemplate the enormous field of service; so many needs and a scant few who would work with dedication! Much to do and so little time to fulfill the quota of the 'calling' in just one short incarnation. The time draws near too quickly when we must surrender the torch of Light to him that follows and I prayed: "God, let me carry these thoughts into my next existence, let me remember Thy Cause!" When suddenly my footless spirit stood at the tip of a great vortex of oscillating, shimmering Light. Within its bluish-white radiance stood the broad, majestic frame of the Teacher. As He streched out His hand toward me the Guiding Love and Tenderness of the Great Unseen drew me swiftly into His Presence. Our ascent was quick and the country we entered most familiar.

Snowcapped Cosmic Mountains of collossal dimensions towered high into an as yet dimly lit star-studded sky. The dreamy song of Cosmic foothills, woods and flowing streams rose upward from far below where scattered hamlets layed in the artistry of nature graced by the rosy-glow of the evening hour. Mighty outbranched oaks silhoutted tall against the deepening evening sky, casting their lengthening shadows over the heavenly landscape, abound with riches and the treasures of inspiration.

We left the panoramic site of murmuring streams that ran into the sea. Across the harbor great beacon lights cast their beams across quiet, velvety waters and the star-jeweled midnight sky now poured down the Melody of God. I perceived that the spirit of fish and foul listened intently, felt the energy-brush of invisible wings and beheld the glorious Presences of the Spirits of the Waters, of Fire, Earth and Air. By the Sound of Heaven a mighty breeze rippled through the waters, as the Breath of God stirred up the waves they now hummed, danced and leaped against the glistening whiteness of reefbound shores and the soft rebounding echo caught me up and the Voice of Him Whom I loved spoke out from the deep of my own heart: "May the Soul bend its ear and listen to My Word! Man cannot divide the Spirit of God and confine it to the narrow compartments of his chosen beliefs, since It is free. Man is bound and enslaved by himself, only the Spirit of God can free him. Man does not choose God, the Eternal chooses him, when the soul decides it is ready. Only when man desires God more than food, drink, aye, I say, more than his very life, only then can the inner meeting take place. Thereafter his opinions, beliefs and creeds no longer matter for the truth has no place in them. No matter what the belief and chosen ideal, each soul shall meet the Christ—the Light-that embodies the Twin-Flame of Light and Sound. In Him—the IT-ye find the Love and Perfection ye seek. The Light is Christ, it is the Spirit of Wisdom, Strength and Truth, the Energy of God that alone delivereth out of bondage. The wondrous Light ye behold in thine forehead, aye, I say, ye are Its reflection and the Light."

My Voice speaketh aloud to the deaf ear: "Harken, be still and know—" that the enticing and warring of the tempter would be closed off, but man is too busy to listen. Introspection, the realization of the Self holds the answer, for only as ye enter the Silence shall the Light appear, clear understanding of Cosmic Law received, to slay thine illusions into remnants by true Realization of the Eternal, the Hidden One, and of thine own Self.

Many who would serve the Christ work with reckless abandon as tho' there were no time for recognizance. Unresolved doubts and perplexities dog their footsteps, hurt and despair take a great toll, for their vision of God is limited, they know not the Way to Love and Perfection and thus they are trapped by their suspicions, superstitions and suppositions as their intellect tears apart the teachings We grant. The haughty mind blocks out the Word, the Sound. Truth has no place in them for they are neither 'hot nor cold,' the fearful mind shuts it out. Such individuals leave many hopes, dreams and deposits to be realized in the next existence until the Soul in self-willed obedience, yea, in LOVE, kneels at the Foot of the Living Spirit and hears none other. All else is folly and their goodness is a compound of virtue and vice. Ye claim ye are purified by devils, but workers of the Shadow are higher than man. Even as God made man 'a little lower than the angels' the Shadow is a tool of Arcane Love. As long as ye dwell in the thought of beliefs ye cannot receive spiritual freedom. Man must close the outer ear to hear the inner Sound of the Spirit of God that alone opens the Gate of Consciousness and permits the Soul to take flight through the Open Door to enter the Kingdoms while ye are still embued by the flesh. For how can ye enter through it if ye never sought it? How can the seed grow if it was never sown?

"My Scribe, hold this ever before thee, that He Who holds the destiny of all watches over thee. As the sparrow cupped in His Hand, so thine Light, thine own True Self thrives and grows in His Palm, until He lets go to catch it up unto Himself as ye step through the Gate of Heaven. And here all thine groping, weeping and wonderments shall find an end in the Love that awaiteth thee and one and all. Until then let there be Peace and utter Trust and the Peace of God rest upon all. Ye have come a great length into the Light, ploughed the furrow well, but much within thee is left unfinished, shall be redeemed, as ye continue to walk in the Light of Love and Perfection.

"As the Son of Man became the Christ, so likewise shall every soul reach the state of Glory that obliterates sorrow, pain and want as ye know it now. And I say unto thee, be strong, of good courage and the Light ye follow and love shall go before and make straight the way. I say, My Beloved, walk in it. Look neither left, nor to the right, but keep the eye of Soul ever on Him, Who is the Light, the Way and the Comforter to all. Ye are as strangers in a strange land, outwardly lonely for ye have been inwardly set apart. Think upon hope, not hopelessness. Oh, My Children of Earth, I would ye might continue walking in the narrow, lighted Way and harm shall not befall nor come neigh thee—walk upright I say, in Grace, honesty, in confidence, knowing in all things He shall bear thee up into the Heart of the Father and ye shall know thine Redeemer liveth and loveth thee as ye have also loved Him.

"And now, that ye have come into the Light of Truth there shall be a new Way made, a new door open and a new dawning for the Soul of humanity. And my Word sent into each purpose shall bear fruit, and accomplish that unto which I sent it. For unto this end ye were born, to do , to dare, to face each challenge of life in confidence and to conquer the small, petty self; for self-conquest sets free from binding ways that keep the soul earthbound. That being free, the eagle may soar to sublime heights and the spirit in man enter the Kingdom of Heaven.

"And I say unto thee, forsake the ties of man, they are weak, come unto Me, lean on Me, I shall grant understanding. Trust, I shall deliver, believe and have faith. Thine desires I grant when ye learn to define between want and need, and then perhaps not in thine expectations. What ye have is what ye need, what ye lack in material ways is to thine benefit, that the soul would remember its Maker and unfold in the riches of God. Doubt not, be at peace!

"Ye are of Noble Birth, of noble estate, but ye forget the manner in which ye were sired and the manners of the Household in which ye were reared by the Gods.

"Fetch now the cool Pitcher of Living Grace and pour Its Waters upon parched lips and hearts. Let the soul rejoice in its labors and the Smile of Heaven shall grace thy pathways. Be at peace, make merry!

"Go now, My Scribe, pen down My Sayings and when the

Shadow casts its gloom over the sunfilled meadow of the heart, turn to Me again and I shall grant *PEACE!"*

Blessings—Grace—*MASTER*—Y.—

A streak of brilliant Light swiftly moved across the face of the Soul, I had returned from a journey with the Master. Ah, yes, I shall gather up His Words and the Light and pass it on to all who would listen to the Voice and the Song of the Spirit.

Chapter Nine

Bells of Freedom

Dictation of June, 1977

America, a Focal Point of Light

Mighty Beings and Intelligences watch over the destiny of nations. Appointed by God, they often bring readjustment when national issues get out of hand and They turn the tide into more favorable directions.

Planetary Servers are equally concerned. They drop pearls of enlightment into our consciousness, pertaining to the welfare of the world. Such a Guardian came into my contemplation and here is what He said:

"Greetings, O Children of Earth! Can you hear the Bells of freedom sounding out peace from the Electrical ethers of Cosmos into the world? What wonderful Sounds...! Ye who are blessed to live in the Americas that is Mother to many nations and a Focal Point of Cosmic Light upon earth, ye are dissatisfied with thy government! I ask what good is a government without the Governorship of Christ? Pray, I say, that the Voice of Freedom would redeem the minds and hearts of your leaders, only then shall peace be re-instated and thy land break the bread of true brotherhood with every nation. Pray, God-Government would be established within every heart to avert a great destruction before the turn of the century! The dissonant sounds of war are welling up, what goes up must come down! Psychic fog obscures the threshold of Light.

"Pray O Children, to whom the Sword and Armor Light is entrusted, for *PEACE, PEACE, G0LDEN PEACE,* that would extinguish the fires of hate, oppression, torment, and material greed of the powerful and unjust; that Peace would clean up mind-pollution and the very air ye breathe! Pray that America would regain strength, security and its innate greatness. Children of Freedom, be not as those who cry easy, dry easy and die easy, but forge ahead in Freedom's Flame to aid thy country that is the Focal Point of Light upon earth; for the searing Flame of Love in action is the only Victor over the turbulent conditions thy country presently endures. These pressures have mounted of long ago and the time does come when love and prayer can no longer suppress the fury and the lid must blow off the pressure kettle!

"Be ye mindful, O Children of Freedom, a Great Dragon shall seek to overtake the Americas, flap its wings over the land. Heed my forewarnings, watch thy borders, Beloved, watch thy borders! Pray thy leaders would keep vigil! The one coming from the East in brotherly gesture to rescue the crumbling economy shall wear the robe of the Great Whore, the Liar, trust him not! Raise thy sight to the God of all, to the Shores from whence deliverance cometh.

"Keep watchful vigil, passing the torch of Freedom one to the other when ye tire, I repeat, watch the borders of the land, East, West, North and South, for the Americas heretofore an example of Light shall see far greater tribulations than are evidenced at present; thieves and opposition shall draw near from countries ye least expect. Believe him not who says all is well, for all is not well, Beloved Torch-Bearers. Atomic warfare shall not cease as long as man is at war with the atoms of his own being.

"Peace cannot be when leaders of your government shake hands in vacillation with other nations, without standing their ground behind the specifics of their demand. Other nations shall not push the buttons of deadly radiation, but they shall continue in cold warfare of which ye know not of, in brotherly pretense and by clever design and maneuvering to overtake America the beautiful. Keep thy vigil, the tyrant cometh from the East. Be watchful for destruction that cometh even *before* the end of your century, and shall usher in a new cycle. Let this forewarning of utter devastation be averted through prayer, visualization of Peace, supplication and a command that shall bring the answer, for He said: 'Command thou Me!'

"Be ye conditioned by the Light of Spirit to be granted protection from the burning, seering Breath that shall pour forth from the Mouth of the Angel that loosens the Seal, that shall pour through the earth world to fulfill a prophecy in midst of a death-cry and famine. I prophesy not that ye should fear and despair, but that ye might be prepared. Ye are not bearers of a weak flame, but of a Flame of Power by which ye may lift the Aquarian Water-Pitcher to pour cooling Love upon parched hearts, I say, unless ye do thine uttermost to raise the life-flame of humanity to enter the new cycle of the Aquarian Age, the earth-world shall annihilate itself, by itself, of itself, not the Globe as it were but all that it embodies. Man has set destructive movements into motion long before ye set foot upon this planet and a time for reaping the full harvest is near. For in the disintegration and corruption of unleashed actions, each rotation shall be more devastating than the last. And now the earth world is experiencing cataclysms in various territories, that bring famine, hunger and thirst upon the unjust and the just. All man has sown in the past is now being realized.

"The servers of the Light are bearing the burdens of undoing, and in this way they carry 'the sins of their forefathers,' for they also lived of yore and corrupted and this is why in doing good the cross seemeth exceedingly heavy, for ye must endure and carry it for all the rest in Global Karma. In the future, as ye perceive time, mayhaps in millions of years, the earth world shall re-enter the Great Galaxy and its flaming core become the sun of a new planet, but ye shall not see it and at that time the earth shall be *THAT* bottomless pit that flameth in the everness of fire, until it exits into space. The sun itself is cool, the earth containeth the heat, a hell as man shouts from pulpits does not exist, is a monumental waste of time, he endeavors to snatch the wretch from a fiery furnace that the cold above and cold below cannot sustain. Pray, Beloved Light-Bearers for the Coming of the Light, the Christ, to some He has already come and He shall come again to receive thee unto Himself.

"The pestilence, sorrow and sickness that plague humankind are the backflow of its own returning actions and not the vengeance of a wrathful God. Man is the avenger! His hate, malice and cruelty hurled corruption into every atomic structure that must come back in like manifestation as malignant forces gather momentum and lower back into world-ethers in forms of hurricanes, typhoons, tidal waves, wars, and pestilence of every sort by which man suffers."

Energy Crisis

"I shall now answer thy questions on energy; when ye learn God IS energy, ye discover God and energy within the self and have come nearer to the answer. Energy composes, diffuses every atom of human flesh, of divinity and of earth. There is no shortage of energy as is believed, energy is Life and that Life is abundance. Ye believe Atomic Energy is the answer? I say not! And what is? Ye look for something that already exists. Heavenly energy is man's supply, but ye say: How can we keep cool in the heat and warm in the cold? When energy is depleted? Who depleted energy? MAN.

"When he ceases to destroy and corrupt the Bounties of Nature, the earth shall in slow process replenish itself and the firmament and opposing poles of earth now out of kilter shall draw back into perfect balance and supply the heat and coolness ye desire by its abundant mass of released energy. How can the earth restore itself? Then ponder from whence all bounty is given and forget not it giveth to the earth-crust alike. And though depletion is evident in its outer courts, in its bosom deep it holds the vaults of overabundant energy supply, unaccessible to man until the time when payment for his destructive actions has been rendered. Ye cannot destroy and not suffer likewise. And then the earth shall let its bounty rise toward its surface and release its sustaining treasures without too much struggle to man. And here ye understand the meaning of My Exhortation that all would abandon their evil ways, not one—but all if it would turn the Hand of Fate. This is the *ONLY* answer to the energy problem of the world. Science upon earth does not grasp the whole truth, for it seeth it not in the Unseen, and it would be quick to refute My Sayings.

"The air shall never be as clear, nor the earth so magnetic as on thy Day of Peace, when Peace shall flow down into the realms of they world, worlds without end, and pour down God-Harmony from Eternal Springs of Creation that evil be wiped off the face of the earth. Ye can hear the Choirs of Peace even now, singing through the cove of the heart as ye move thy inner flame into action. Rise up, I say, girded with courage in defense of the land in which ye live. Mark ye well, unity of nations and peace of mind are wrought by unity in Spirit. Take up thine armor to clear the way for a Great Replenishing of the Planet, what assaileth one member of the universal body or graces it, affects every other Light-System and member of the Whole. I say, ye can prevent it, the ruin of thy nation. If ye are strong enough, brave enough, pray enough and do enough in the service to the Righteous Cause in the right application of Divine Law, America shall redeem itself, restore itself and be blessed.

"America, the Focal Point of Light, has magnified abundance since thine Elder Brothers set foot on its platform and found there the Bounties of God. And in the Mark of the Cosmic Christ it shall be raised, by the Finger of God it shall be plucked up out of the mire; in unity of loving souls it shall rise again, propelled by the Powers of Light. For, 'ye have loved not in word, neither in tongue, but in deed and in truth.'

"Listen to Our Counsel, pen Our Dispensations, by which ye may channel forth the Great Light that fortifies souls upon earth and the land ye dwell in. And while to some the Light flickers from afar, it is nearer to thee, O Beloved of Christ, nearer than hand and foot. May the Blessing Be, *PEACE!*"

I AM A GUARDIAN OF EARTH
I AM
—SUDHAR SINGH—

Virgin of Light

Divine Intelligences fortify and teach us in The Way, they leave with us a glow of innate happiness, a sense of belonging to a Great family that cares for each soul. I've received the benediction of the Blessed Lady not by virtue but Grace. Her last Appearance was only days before the earthquake demolished parts of Maysville, Kentucky, in 1980. The reality of the experience is presented in other writings*. The directive in Her Message is a rather personal one since it pertains to my work and is shared with my Reader to prove the reality of Divine Contact regardless of our beliefs or creed. The Divine not only speaks to servers but also to those who never had religious training. I've met persons whose humility was infilled with Grace, they had a quiet, infinite way about them that would perplex the parson. The underlying reason of a Holy Manifestation may elude us but we may be sure it is for infinite purposes. Her spoken word was accompanied by colorful visions and as any other teacher she gently counseled me to tow the line. She began with a sentence in Latin and continued:

*See *Journeys to Worlds Beyond*, Carlton Press, Inc., N.Y., N.Y.

"Those who would serve the Master, let them arise from their bed and serve. Procastination is a game, a dangerous game that debilitates all will, earnest contentions and enthusiasm. I say not that ye should strive My Children, but to know thy work and purposes in thy sojourn through earth. Tarry not to fulfill the Law, the work He has set before thee, rid thyself of excess materialism in that ye neither acquire nor add to thine estate for it shall be a hindrance in going places pointed out to thee. Be not hesitant to venture out alone, I shall be in the purpose unto which I send thee. Ye shall not sit with men of ill repute, neither talk in their tongues, lest ye be drawn into their nets to perish, deterred from thy purpose that must come into completion in thy present incarnation that would close thy present evolutionary round as ye shall continue teaching in Higher Octaves after ye have left the flesh.

"What distrubeth thee? I have sent thee out to speak, to deliver a Message of the Great Light, ye seek to withdraw? I say, words shall drop into the heart like dew-drops upon the satin crown of a rose, Grace pour down from Above to benefit the listener, dread not but rejoice. Ye must walk in confidence, honor and strength to intensify the virtue that fulfills the Law. What ye suffered of late We permitted to purify the vessel, prepare it for better service that We deem shall not bring thee gold as man desires, but that the Light shall shine forth into the hearts of men. Ye shall continue to serve Him as in the days of thine first commitment when His Light fell upon the vow and promise of thy Love for Him, to serve Him in humility.

"In thy present procrastinations ye tend to dilute the context of My Sayings, carelessly laying it aside. Ye must redeem again, to present thyself to God in readiness to follow the furrow the Light prepared. Thus, the body is weakened by necessity which does not please Me, some only listen through pain, it shall be thy blessing in the end. Fasten thy gaze upon Me, in retrospect reliving this day of My Countenance, it shall bring forth the vision, the Light, and when in desolation thine heart parched with tears ye call forth My Name, with the same Heart I shall answer knowing the pain. And ye shall do as it is given and accept what is set before thee by Cosmic Mandate and ye shall serve, create, in clear perception of deep, pure Love, loving God. Thus ye shall pick up an old order left unfinished heretofore and serve man and creature in the place unto which I shall send thee.

"Go ye East unto the mountains, east of the great city by the Great Waters that murmur and cry in warning of coming desolations while its waves crash against rocky shores and reef, where white foam of tears unseen seep into the sands, O, that man would listen with his heart! Clouds of darkness slowly gather their cloak about the world or carnal man, soothsayers, workers of iniquity and the self that misplaced all virtues of life and threw them into the melting pot of evil. A new Dawn is upon your world. Go ye, teach the Way of Light, of Higher Being, of Higher Worlds, for on that dark day when the cold, dead fog of carnal emotions covers the earth, the unendurable Whiteness of the Son of Light, the Brilliance of His Glory shall pierce the thickest of all carnality and blot out evil. And the Light of His Countenance shall shine into the deepest recess of thine heart and hold thee accountable in all things, unto the vaguest thought ye shall render account. For unto thee has been given a great gift, therefore responsibility must be greater.

"I gave instructions, the impulse as of long ago, and ask thee to do so of late, to make an abode for those in need, in all things We shall provide. And in thy radiant purpose thy spirit shall be cleansed white as driven snow and the Rose of Love rest upon its altar, that ye may roll away the stone of many tombs. And then I say, go ye unto the fields, the woods, let thy spirit roam through natural quietudes unto the High, White Mountain of God, to bathe the soul in its quickening springs. In meadowed outer court in the place I shall send thee, the abode shall be. I ask not ye should lavish all thine earthly good unto it as would be thy natural promptings, but rather to fill it with the radiant love ye are capable of giving, to let My Grace be unto thee that ye might continue bearing the burdens of Light. My Grace is unto thee, O Child, thy hands shall bleed as of yore when ye stood in fright of the happening and sting. When man scoffed thine account, thine heart withdrew in coldness and that ye must now again bring into submission.

"Fear not, I say, Angels shall carry the silver Chalice into thine aid, those vials charged with the empowerment of His Light, that ye even now receive, make use of in the restoration of those in need. And these, My Requests I now lay upon thy shining self in the Benediction of the Redeeming Christ, as I spoke so shall it be! A Rose—

"A Light—

"And a Blessing in that ye may rejoice, this I grant to one and all."

—I AM—
—MARY—

Guardian of the Heart

The soft voice of the Angel draws into our solitude. My evening hour was graced as the Radiant Guardian of the Heart appeared saying:

"I *AM* come in the Light, I speak out of the deep of your innermost Self. There is need for supplication, let not thy faith falter as the outer self gives in to worldly want. The impermanence of the material world, the gold of Mammon, can bring perdition to the seeker. Albeit changes are slow, they do come! The body must seek rest in nature to keep balance, the Life Force for the Eternal in its green bounty fortifies body and soul, the twain must harmonize, else the mind gives off a note of warning by manifesting unease in outer conditions. Erase inharmony, pluck it up as a weed out of the garden of soul and Peace, Sweet Peace shall quickly find you.

"My unfailing Guidance, My Presence walks ever near, hearing, caring and knowing all you do. I have always been with you, from age to age, *I AM* there. Whether you stepped forward, backward or off the path, it was I, your Guardian Spirit that pulled you back into the Light. It was My Light, that led you out of desolation into success and at times I had to leave you to suffer the failures of your own willfulness; yet I lured you back by Visions of heaven and unto the Way that leads home to the Father's House. Even in your intoxications of wordly pleasures and unworthy conduct, I was there, not withholding My Guidance. I was there in your weakness, pain, bereavements, and in your disgust and tears you reached for Me again and I gave Guidance.

"My Voice in your conscience would not permit you to rest until a wrong was made right, until the hands of your heart ripped at My Garment in the remorse of self-undoing. I have set you aglow with inspiration, with every determination in your leaving, loving and caring, that in My Guidance you would set My Will into action to dare and to do! In your joys and labors, in your awesome temptations and self-denials I have always been with you. *I AM* the Guardian of many hearts. My Guiding Light shines out from the deep peace of every soul, if you desire, you can find Me! I soften and ease the pain and paths of many creatures, be it My Touch upon a flower, a leaf, a tree, weed or stone, or upon the outcrying heart of fowl or beast, My Guidance appears in many ways, *I AM* there.

"In your being I stand as a shaft of Light, I keep vigil in your night and turn the Key to Heaven Doors that your spirit may enter. All these I do in the everness of our bond. *I AM* the Angel before the Throne for every soul, Who stood in every phase of your life, for *I AM YOURSELF!* Nothing remains concealed. I guide the poor in spirit, the weakest vessel grows strong in the refining Light of My Love. And as you pray for peace, may it find you! But I would you might rather pray for discontent, that in holy discontent you would forsake the small patch of grass at the rim of the hill and climb the White Mountain of self-perfection to Peace Everlasting! My Light leads you unto the Path of all paths, when the cup you carry becomes empty of all unholiness. *I AM forever* with you, for *I AM YOURSELF.*"

—*I AM* Eternally—
—*THE GUARDIAN OF YOUR HEART*—

And here, I, the Scribe, lay down the pen of my heart, the Angel Voice fell silent for the day and Dialogues and Holy Dispensations withdrew into Golden-White Mist. And as I bade Them farewell, the Angel turned to me in Blessing:

> "Enter the Silence and remove all doubt. Leave the sandals of your being at the threshold of the Temple of Peace before you enter, that Wisdom may be the experience of the Soul and Truth be found in the heart filled with Grace. May the Light of Love overshadow, may the Blessing Be, and the dew of Inspiration remain upon your crown. May Peace, Golden *PEACE* and the Harmony of Christ be with you now, and forevermore."

Conclusion: The Way of Love

When Truth finds homage in the heart, man's ordinary state

of consciousness enters the transformation that unfolds his highest potentials as a human-being and a soul. The focus exalts inner living, selfless service, spiritual freedom, right government of thought, inner growth, and spiritual peace, for the soul has set foot upon the Royal Highway that leads back home to God. He perceives the constantly overshadowing Presence of the Guiding Master Spirit and begins to live in the Eternal *NOW* in the very life he lives.

God's Divine Regents are Masters of Perfection, Masters over the elements and powers of nature, they link to the purest, highest aspect of regenerated man to aid, counsel and to direct the soul on its ascent to the Worlds of God. Every step taken under their Guiding Force is vital to inner unfoldment as you walk through the regeneration, clear, translucent Water of the Spirit of Light. Should you stumble, remember you can only rise or fall and should you fall you shall quickly rise again, stronger, better and wiser for the experience.

Too many follow earth masters in blind faith, know, a true Master is recognized by the pure life he lives, he is free of criticism, asks nothing, never displays authority nor position—but kindles the light within many hearts, that truth, joy and the flow of heavenly power would instill the spiritual potency and fire that alone can burn away the personal self. A true Master serves without thought of reward. Many there be that walk among us who live among the lowly and downtodden, the Light of their pure force-field shines as a thousand suns, for the Living Flame of Christ shines in brightness. This is the destiny of every soul—to regain its divinity. To come apart from material greed we find renunciation brings stillness and peace, without it you cannot live the spiritual life and how can we help others find it when we have not found peace within ourselves? When discord, pain and agony have run its course on body and mind, the personality will finally turn away and seek peace at any cost. Only then can a life of peace manifest for harmony and peace are the Way of Love, not longsuffering! Peace is not found in outward place, it begins in the center of your true divinity and sheds its light into your outer life. Then you shall look far beyond the world's transitory pleasures and magnify virtue everlasting, the Virtue of God. Keep the virtue that faces the Sun of Light and the pavements of your life shall become cushioned carpets of greens, the hillsides, valleys, and gardens of the soul shall reverberate a blessing to every selfless deed, and the morning dew shall lay like pearls of Glory across the meadows of the heart, born of your loving, giving as your every thought and action are rendered in the Name of God.

You believe in the spiritual life? You may live it, it is yours for the taking but not without effort, action, detachment, supplications and self-willed surrender to the Spirit of God. As you "lift your eyes unto the hills" your conscience approves, corrects and warns, for the Consciousness of God is within *YOU*. As you live in the Way of Love, claim Love in your waking hours, Love shall betide your sleep, you shall know none other, and it shall not matter how much you loved, but how purely. Then the tenderness and guidance of God's Shining Hosts shall aid your every cause and you shall know the Great Unseen is your True Reality.

The spiritual life is not static but dynamic. It is realized through the acquisition of inward reverence, daily contemplation upon the Light in preparation to meet the Inner Master. Then the Sound shall bear you up and you shall no longer believe or assume for you shall know what *IS*, and because *God IS*—you *ARE*. This shall free you from all outer worship as you go to the Throne of Light within to find: man is law unto himself and reaps what he sows. Man has no soul, he *IS* the *SOUL*.

Deepest Truth is garnered by coming apart from haste and anxieties and in active contemplation entering the Stillness, the Great Silence that lifts the weary wanderer into the sunlit worlds of God to experience the Reality of Heavenly Countries and the irrepressible joy only He can give. To travel the Royal Highway of innate happiness, spiritual laws applied to the Self and not to others. Then the Soul-Light shall grow bright and strong "as a light set upon a hill" that illumines all darkness.

Christ IS Lord, for Christ is the Light and very life of God you see within your forehead as you deeply pray. You are a Spark of this Living Light that came into this world to perfect its lesser being, the personality. Soul is a Light of Fire, it cannot be annihilated, it is immortal, the Eternal *YOU*.

And finally, when the Way of Love instilled Its Living Word to the heart, you shall hear these self-same words the Master of Light spoke to me of long ago:

"Come apart, lean on Me, I will give you understanding. Trust, I shall deliver, believe and have faith. Have courage, go onward, forsake the ties of man, they are weak, I say, so is their understanding. Thy desire I grant, mayhaps not to thine expectations. I give what is needed, doubt not! Be at Peace—Be still and know—*I AM God*—"

Blessings—Grace—*THE MASTER*